Red Fox Running

Red Fox Running

ROBIN LLOYD-JONES

Andersen Press • London

For Chloe, Cassandra and Andre with love

First published in 2007 by
Andersen Press Limited,
20 Vauxhall Bridge Road, London SW1V 2SA
www.andersenpress.co.uk

British Library Cataloguing in Publication Data available
ISBN 978 184 270 552 0

Poem from
Seasons of the Eskimo: A Vanishing Way of Life by Fred Bruemmer,
published by McClelland & Stewart Ltd. © 1971.
Reprinted with permission from the publisher.

[illegible] Books, Enfield, Middx.
Printed and bound in Great Britain by
[illegible]yman, R[illegible]ading, Berkshire

Acknowledgements

I would like to thank all those who have supported and encouraged me in writing this book, in particular: Moris Farhi, Sallie Lloyd-Jones, Douglas Mackenzie, Jim Muir, Deborah Nelken, and the many members of Helensburgh Writers' Workshop who, at various times, commented on various chapters. My thanks also go to the Scottish Arts Council whose generous grant funded the necessary research, and to Elizabeth Maude of Andersen Press for her helpful and sensitive editing and for all her work in seeing this story into print.

Chapter One

The bear was gaining on Adam. Its low growl, so close behind, made him plunge wildly through the snow. He tried to run, but the snow was deep and soft. He was sinking up to his knees with every pace. He was wading uphill now, floundering, slipping backwards. He felt the bear's hot breath on the back of his neck. Adam sat up with a jerk, breathing hard . . . That same dream again!

Through the uncurtained window in the attic he could see thickets of masts swaying in the cold moonlight. Along the quayside were idle carts, piles of barrels, heaps of coal, and the shops and yards of coopers, sailmakers, riggers and a host more. Skug was asleep in the other bed.

This is going to be the worst birthday I've ever had, Adam thought.

Today, April the 10th, he was sixteen. This day, a year ago, he had sat down beside a warm fire to a birthday cake with icing and candles. It seemed impossible to imagine now, but he'd been cross about the cake because candles had seemed too childish for a fifteen-year-old. His mouth watered at the thought of the cake sweetly clinging to the roof of his mouth, softly sliding down his throat, filling his stomach. He imagined he was cutting the first slice and making his wish. He wished for the same thing he had wished for every year since he was thirteen – that his father would return; that, somehow, he had survived when his ship sank.

There had been only two survivors when the whaler, *Triton,* struck an iceberg in Baffin Bay. Missing, presumed drowned, was the official verdict on Nathaniel Jones. Presumed – it meant they didn't really know what had happened to him. It left just enough doubt, just enough hope for Adam to raise his head every time he heard footsteps on the cobbles outside his window, and for his heart to miss a beat when, in the distance, he sighted a mane of red hair. Panic surged through him. Suppose his father came looking for him at Aunt Emily's place? Adam had returned several times to the little red-brick terrace house. He had left a message saying he was now living with his uncle on the new Victoria Dock. But the last time he went back, there'd been a new tenant who knew nothing about him.

When Aunt Emily realised her end was near, she had made Uncle Jeremiah Jones take Adam on as an apprentice. So Adam was learning the chandlery trade, which involved supplying ships with just about everything they needed for a long voyage. Jeremiah's house was joined to his shop. After the funeral, Jeremiah had grudgingly taken Adam back with him and let him share a small attic room with Skug, an apprentice from the orphanage. Nobody knew Skug's real name.

Skug was nearly two years older than Adam, with big knuckles, hard knees and sharp elbows, all well practised in inflicting pain on Adam. Uncle Jeremiah had taken Skug on because he didn't have to pay him. Board and lodging was good enough for an orphanage boy... and for a relative given a roof over his head out of charity. According to Jeremiah's maid-of-all-work, Skug's father had been a lascar, an Indian seaman, and his English mother had died in the workhouse.

The day usually began with Skug hurling a boot at him. If Skug found out it was his birthday, he'd most likely get sixteen kicks on the backside for a present. At least there was no danger of Uncle Jeremiah letting on about it. He always forgot, even when Aunt Emily had been alive to remind him. A clock on the north side of the Thames boomed five. Adam decided to get up before Skug was awake. He lit a candle and shivered his way to the china jug and basin in the corner. He examined his spots in the cracked mirror. There was a boil on the side of his neck and his face was a mass of red lumps. He squeezed the big one on the side of his nose, but it was unyielding and only became more angry. Why, he wondered, was there no sign of hair on his lip or chin? Adam filled the basin, shut his eyes and splashed his face with the icy water. Something soft and soggy pressed against his mouth. He opened his eyes to see a dead mouse in his cupped hands. Behind him Skug was crowing with triumph and waving the empty mousetrap.

'Got you!' he jeered.

Adam emptied the basin over him. Gasping and spluttering, Skug grappled Adam to the floor and sat astride him, pinning his arms with his knees. Dangling the mouse by its tail, he gripped Adam's jaw, trying to force his mouth open.

'You're going to eat it!'

'Not!' Adam hissed through clenched teeth.

The pain of Skug's fingers pressing into his jaw muscles was almost unbearable. The attic door opened. Jeremiah glared down at them.

'What are you two doing?'

'Nothing,' Skug muttered, standing up.

Jeremiah smacked Skug across the head. 'You know very well we're shifting the *Prince Consort*'s supplies today. Didn't I tell you I wanted you both on the job early?... Well, didn't I?'

'Yes,' the two boys mumbled.

'Instead I find you up to some tomfoolery. Is this how you repay me for taking you in when nobody else would have you and teaching you a trade?'

Adam and Skug looked at each other and said nothing.

'I suppose I should have known what to expect, considering the kind of parents you both had!'

'There's nothing wrong with my parents!' Adam shouted, scrambling to his feet.

'Oh, if I hadn't promised your aunt, I could tell you a tale or two... It's getting late. If you're not down in five minutes you can go without breakfast!' Jeremiah turned towards the door. 'Half-baked trash!' he growled and slammed the door behind him.

'All your fault getting his rag up like that,' Skug said, punching Adam on the arm.

Adam retaliated. 'Half-baked trash! Half-baked half-caste!'

He was heading for the window even before his taunt had passed his lips. He didn't know why that was such a bad thing to be. He just knew that people thought it was and that he could hurt Skug by saying it. Leaning out and grasping the gutter overhead, he swung upwards, got a purchase with his heel and pulled himself onto the roof. He squatted on the sloping tiles. He knew Skug's weak spot, his fear of heights. He wouldn't try to follow.

Skug's upturned face stared up at him, fury and misery stamped upon it. 'You'll be sorry, you'll see!'

Adam and Skug carried a wooden box across the yard, ignoring each other as much possible. Adam had missed breakfast, but it had been worth it. He didn't often get a chance to score off Skug. In an old fisherman's sweater which hung loosely from his shoulders and came down to his knees, Adam felt drab compared to Skug. The latter sported a stove-pipe hat and two coats, one on top of the other, in green and blue, one buttonless, one sleeveless, and with holes that didn't quite coincide so that, between them, they contrived to meet the normal expectations of a coat. The quartermaster of the *Prince Consort* directed the boys to put the box on a cart which six seamen were preparing to haul away.

Jeremiah Jones, Ships' Chandlers, had secured a big order from the Royal Navy. The *Prince Consort* was moored nearby and was taking on stores in preparation for an Arctic expedition.

Strictly speaking, the *Prince Consort* was a barque, with

a foremast, a mainmast and a mizzenmast at the stern. The vessel had been specially built to withstand the crushing pressure of the ice, with a hull made of three layers of timber. She also had a steam engine and a funnel. Adam and Skug had argued about it. Skug stubbornly maintained the *Prince Consort* was a sailing ship with an auxiliary engine. Adam was sure she was a steamship with auxiliary sails. The newly built ship had been named in honour of Prince Albert, the Queen's husband. Last year, the twenty-first year of her reign, she had bestowed upon him the title of Prince Consort.

According to the newspapers, the expedition's leader was Admiral Charles Burden. The gossip was that he was a vain and ambitious man who had not quite won the fame and glory of some of his contemporaries. His quest was to continue the search for the expedition, led by Sir John Franklin, which had disappeared ten years ago. For a whole decade the search for the two missing ships and their crew had gone on. More than forty expeditions had scoured the central Arctic region without finding a trace of them. Then, three years ago, a Scotsman, John Rae, had returned with relics purchased from a group of Inuit – a watch engraved with the name of one of the officers, a silver spoon embossed with the expedition crest, and a medal belonging to Franklin himself. The Inuit said they'd found thirty bodies in a distant place which, from their description, Rae thought was probably King William Island. Adam remembered reading about it in the newspapers. Anything to do with the Arctic he devoured with a fearful fascination. It always left him disturbed and upset and yet he couldn't stop himself reading and rereading every word printed about the vast white wilderness into which his father, too, had disappeared.

The two boys were kept busy all morning, bringing out the supplies from the storage sheds which surrounded Jeremiah's yard. Twenty or more seamen, supervised by the *Prince Consort*'s quartermaster, were filling carts with sacks, barrels, wooden boxes and canvas bags. There were hogsheads of ale, kegs of lemon juice and casks of flour. Adam humped a crate of tin cans towards the carts. The labels said 'Mock turtle soup'.

'The likes of us will never taste that!' a small, wiry seaman remarked cheerfully enough. 'For hofficers only, that is.'

The tip of the seaman's nose was missing and he had lost a finger and the last joint on two others. Adam had seen the results of frostbite before. His own father had no toes on one foot. That was what the Arctic could do to you.

'How many times have you been North?' Adam asked.

'Volunteered three times for Arctic service. And been north of seventy twice,' the sailor grunted, heaving a sack of split peas onto his shoulder. 'And, for all that, lucky to get signed on this time.'

'Less of the gabbing!' the quartermaster bellowed.

'Aye, aye, sir.' The seaman winked at Adam and displayed a ferret tattooed on the back of his hand. 'Ferret's the name.'

Adam felt a deep fear of the Arctic. It was a deadly place where people drowned, were maimed by frostbite, tortured by scurvy and snow-blindness, and starved or froze to death. It had taken his father and if he, Adam, was ever so stupid as to venture there it would claim him too. And yet, just as the seaman, Ferret, was doing, his father had returned to it again and again, not for the money to be made, but because he couldn't keep away.

Adam took a brown shellac case from his trouser pocket in which was mounted, not a daguerreotype like the ones on Aunt Emily's mantelpiece, but the superior collodion photograph. Harpoon in hand, a younger Adam stood beside his father: Adam, small for his age and dark, with straight black hair; his father, well-built, with an arm resting on his son's shoulder. Although the picture was in black and white, you could somehow tell his father's beard and thick mane of hair were red. Adam recalled with a lurch of his heart how proud he'd been to be 'pictured off' next to his father, the renowned spectioneer – a harpooner, the key man on any whaler. Proud, but also scared, because that was the day his father had put into words what had, until then, been unspoken – that he expected Adam to follow in his footsteps. . . The photograph was snatched from his grasp. Skug was dancing in front of him, threatening to sling it over the wall.

'Don't!' Adam howled. 'Please, Skug!'

Skug laughed and mimicked Adam's breaking voice, growling and squeaking and never sure which. Adam lunged for his most valued possession, but Skug held it out of reach. He hurled himself at Skug, butting him in the stomach. Skug fell backwards, dropping the shellac case, his flailing arms knocking over a huge glass jar in a wicker basket. Vinegar spread across the yard. Skug leapt up and grappled with Adam. They rolled amongst the piles of supplies. A scrabbling boot tore open a sack of flour. Clouds of white dust filled the air. A heavy tin of carrots, aimed at Adam, stove in a crate. Ferret and another seaman hauled the two boys apart and held them fast as Jeremiah appeared on the scene of destruction.

'You're sacked!' he screamed at the boys. 'Both of you!'

'But . . .' Adam began.

'Don't but me, you little hooligan!'

'He butted me,' Skug said, grinning slyly at Adam.

Jeremiah turned to the quartermaster and apologised for what had happened. 'Good apprentice boys are harder to find than a sober sailor in a tavern. You have to take what you can get these days, even ones with a touch of the tar-brush.'

He waved angrily at the ruined supplies. 'I want you two gone before tonight!'

Turning on his heel, he stomped off.

'Bad luck, lad,' Ferret said to Adam, handing him his case with the photograph in it. 'You put up a good fight for a shrimp. Tell you what . . . I hear we've gone short of a cabin boy. The poor little blighter went down with chicken pox. If you want a chance at it, better cut along sharpish.'

'Thanks,' Adam said, but what he thought was: Nothing, nothing or nobody will ever persuade me to set foot on that ship.

Chapter Two

It was seven in the morning. Adam's feet felt like lumps of ice as he padded through the frosted streets. He had shivered the long night hours away huddled in a doorway. An old woman was selling roasted nuts beside a brazier of hot coals. He had no money, but at least he could warm himself near the coals. His stomach cramped with hunger. Yesterday he'd earned a few coppers as a crossing sweeper. It was a matter of waiting until a woman of quality wanted to cross the street, then dashing forward and sweeping the horse droppings out of her path, so that she didn't soil her long dress. There was usually a farthing tip in it. He'd made the broom from branches and twigs he'd gathered in the park. The trouble was, bigger boys soon showed up and took over, even tried to get your earnings off you.

'You don't look like a street sparrow,' the old woman said.

Adam shook his head.

'How long you been on the street?'

'Two days.'

'No home to go to?'

Adam shook his head again. Without a relative in the same line of work to speak for you, to buy the foreman a drink or slip him money, he'd have about as much luck as would a rat in a snake-pit. He'd seen seamen fighting to be at the front when crews were picked; and he'd witnessed a man going through the pockets of someone knocked down by a cab, not to steal the money, but to find out where he worked and be the first to apply for the vacancy.

The old woman gave him a hot chestnut. He wolfed it down, burning his tongue. This would have been his morning off if he'd still been working for Uncle Jeremiah. He usually spent at least an hour of his precious free time visiting Aunt Emily's grave. That was what he'd do now. Even from the grave, Aunt Emily seemed able to comfort him.

As he passed through the cemetery gates, head down, hunched against the cold, he all but bumped into a tall, gaunt man, soberly dressed in dark blue. The place was deserted. The man's footprints in the frost led to and from the same part of the cemetery where Aunt Emily was buried – the part where the graves were smaller and more closely packed. The footprints made a sudden right turn – into Aunt Emily's row . . . and halted right beside her grave. Adam's heart lurched. Who but his father would . . . ? No, the man he'd nearly bumped into was not his father, he was certain of that. So who could he be? Adam turned and raced back towards the gates.

On the pavement outside the cemetery the footprints were fast disappearing in the morning sun and other people had passed along that way, obscuring the man's tracks. Which way? He took a guess and went left.

Rounding a bend he saw the tall figure about to step into a horse-drawn cab.

'Sir! Mister! Wait!'

The man hesitated, then waited for Adam to reach him.

'Excuse me, sir,' Adam panted. 'It was you, wasn't it, who was at my aunt's grave?'

The man's deep grey eyes studied him. 'Yes, I see it now. You've got your mother's hair and eyes, but that mouth, that's your father's. You're Adam, Nathaniel Jones's boy, aren't you?'

'Yes, sir.'

'And I am Captain Elisha McLellan. I knew your father well. We sailed together many a time.'

Elisha McLellan explained that he had only recently arrived in London and, on learning of Aunt Emily's death, had gone to her grave to pay his respects.

'You must miss her,' he said.

Adam nodded, fighting the sudden lump in his throat. 'I miss my father, too.'

Elisha put a large bony hand on Adam's shoulder. 'You look as though you could do with a good hot meal inside you.'

He guided Adam into the waiting cab, calling out the name of an eating house to the cabby.

The padded upholstery seemed so soft and inviting.

'Nothing fancy at the *Grub and Grog*,' he said to Adam. 'Good plain fare and helpings to fill even boys with hollow legs.'

While they ate, Elisha drew Adam's story from him with a kind of gruff gentleness that belied his stern features. And Adam, in his turn, learned that Captain Elisha McLellan was the *Prince Consort's* Ice Master, the man who would guide the ship through the pack ice – the drifting, ever-changing sea ice. Elisha did not need to explain to the son of a spectioneer that nobody understood pack ice in all its dangerous moods better than a whaling captain.

'So you have nowhere to sleep and no money and no job?'

The room was so warm and cosy. Adam's head drooped and touched his plate.

'Don't go to sleep yet, lad. There's plum duff still to come . . . I was thinking . . . we're short of a cabin boy.'

'I know. One of the crew told me yesterday.'

'There should be three cabin boys on the ship's complement, but first one, then another, has gone down with something.'

'Chicken pox,' Adam said.

'I believe we've got one replacement, but there's still . . . I could put in a word for you, if you like.'

Adam toyed with his plum duff, his appetite suddenly gone. The Ice Master wouldn't understand if he said he didn't want the job, not the son of the big, brave Nathaniel Jones. He shoved a spoonful of the warm doughy pudding into his mouth to give himself time before he had to reply.

When he finally swallowed, he said, 'Captain McLellan, sir... tell me about my father.'

Elisha told Adam that the last, ill-fated voyage of the *Triton* had been one of the rare occasions he and Nathaniel had set out for Arctic waters on different vessels. Three months ago, Elisha had met one of the few survivors of the *Triton* from whom he had learned that, in fact, Nathaniel did not drown when the whaler sank. He had gone missing before then. He and two companions had set out in a small boat to hunt seals. They had landed on an ice floe which had then split in two, separating Nathaniel from the others. A sea mist had enveloped them and they lost sight of him.

Adam could hardly get the words out. 'So, nobody saw him drown, then? That means he could be... be alive!'

The Ice Master looked deep into Adam's eyes. 'Don't build your hopes too high, Adam. The moment he was adrift and alone on that ice floe the odds were stacked heavily against him.'

'But he could have survived. Somehow, he could have, couldn't he?'

The Ice Master lit a pipe. Curls of blue smoke drifted up to the blackened beams. 'There was a case, about nine years ago, of six men who kept alive on a large ice floe for seven months until they drifted into the shipping routes. And there's been folk given up for dead who have turned up with tales of being found by Eskimos and given food and shelter by them. But, like I said, don't get your hopes up.'

Adam said, 'Will you be going anywhere near where he was last seen?'

'Nothing's certain in those latitudes, Adam, but, yes, I think it's possible we will.' Elisha rubbed his chin with the stem of his pipe. 'Through the Davis Strait and up the west coast of Greenland, that's our intended course. If he's anywhere, that's where he's going to be. But like I said, Adam...'

'I want to do it!' Adam blurted out.

'You mean...'

'Yes, sir. I want to sail with the *Prince Consort*!'

Chapter Three

The cabin was hardly bigger than a wooden crate, Adam thought. It belonged to the young, horse-faced lieutenant in the dark blue officer's uniform who was rubbing his long nose and looking Adam up and down. George Grenier was known to one and all as Horse, having acquired that name because his initials were GG. One half of the tiny cabin was filled by a built-in cradle-sided bunk. A shelf overhead and drawers beneath the bunk provided the only storage space. A whale-oil lamp was fixed to the bulkhead, but, since it was only just past midday, it was unlit. On one wall was a drop-down writing table at which Third Lieutenant Grenier was sitting. He was studying the expedition muster at the back of the logbook, a large leather-bound tome with brass corners. Adam was squeezed up against the washstand, occupying the only remaining space.

'Well, better get you officially signed on,' Horse announced. Adam thought he detected traces of a Yorkshire accent.

'Age?'

'Sixteen.'

'Sixteen, what?'

'Sixteen years.'

Horse coughed and snorted and rocked in his chair, whinnying softly, before bursting out laughing. 'You're supposed to say, "Sixteen, sir."'

He slanted the big book towards Adam, dipped a steel-nibbed pen into an ink-pot and held it out. 'Sign there, or make your mark. And don't blot it.'

Adam wrote his name. Horse nodded approvingly. He took the pen back and added the date – 13th April, 1859.

'Friday the 13th, eh? I hope this isn't going to be an unlucky voyage for you.'

Adam tried to grin to show he knew it was a joke, but his mouth had gone dry and his jaw seemed harder to open than a rusty penknife.

Horse reeled off the duties of a cabin boy: cleaning the officers' cabins and lighting the lamps in the evening, making the officers' beds, emptying their chamber pots, running errands for them, helping the cook in the galley, serving the officers at meal times, and generally making himself useful and keeping out of mischief.

Whatever the duties are, Adam thought, at least Skug won't be here, making things twice as difficult for me. I'll just have the ice and the polar bears instead.

Adam spotted several books about marine engineering lying on the bed. The young lieutenant saw the direction of his gaze and his face clouded. 'It doesn't mean to say I go about all day in greasy overalls, smelling of engine oil.'

He sniffed the back of his hand as if to reassure himself on this point. Adam noticed a large bottle of eau de Cologne on the shelf. Horse seemed to warm to his subject, to get the bit between his teeth.

'Steam power and the new engines are changing this country for ever, making it rich. They are the future, and yet engineering is not considered a nice occupation for a gentleman, not something a person of good breeding would choose to do.' He coughed, embarrassed that he had said too much, and looked relieved when there was a knock on the door.

There was a twinkle in his eye. 'This will be one of the other two cabin boys come to show you round.'

He folded the writing desk back and opened the door. Standing there was . . . not a boy, but a girl with straight dark hair, dressed in a shirt and trousers made from some kind of animal hide, and sealskin boots.

'Meet Pipaluk,' Horse said. 'She's an Eskimo.'

Adam gathered from Pipaluk that the lower deck, which was less than one hundred feet long and thirty feet wide, would be home for sixty-seven men for the next eighteen months or more. Her voice had a slightly thick, guttural quality which, to Adam, sounded exotic and immensely appealing.

'And below us,' she said, 'is the orlop deck, fuller than a hunter's igloo when he has made a catch.'

'Full of what?'

'All his neighbours, of course, enjoying the fresh meat.'

'I meant the orlop deck. What's down there?'

'Food mostly, and coal. And below that is the hold which . . . er . . . holds the engines, the water tanks and more coal . . . What are you staring at?'

Adam was about to say that he'd never seen an Eskimo before, nor had he ever seen a girl wearing trousers, but changed his mind and said, 'How did you learn to speak English so well?'

Pipaluk recounted how, nearly three years ago, she and her uncle, Ululik, had met up with an expedition of qallunaat.

'What's that?'

'White men. People like yourself. We went on board their ship to trade.'

'What sort of things?'

'We had furs. They had nails, needles, tobacco, tea, iron, wood and other useful things we did not have.'

'My father brought back a bearskin once. Aunt Emily used it as a rug.'

'They set sail while we were still aboard.'

'That's kidnapping!'

Pipaluk frowned. 'I do not know that word.'

Adam explained. Pipaluk shrugged. 'Ululik agreed, in the end. The leader was Charles Burden, the same person who is the leader of this expedition. He persuaded my uncle to go with them across the great ocean to see the land where the qallunaat live.'

'What about your parents, Pipaluk. Shouldn't someone have asked them?'

Pipaluk paused with her hand on the door of a cabin at the very stern of the *Prince Consort*.

'They are both dead, so I lived with my two uncles.'

'I lived with my uncle, too.'

Pipaluk opened the door and they stepped into a cabin, larger than the others, lined with books. There were books about navigation, naval history and Arctic exploration alongside copies of *Punch* and stacks of testaments and prayer books. Adam noticed a shelf full of the works of Charles Dickens, including his latest one, *Little Dorrit*, which Aunt Emily had read aloud to him, only a few months before she died. And there were piles of reading primers and exercise books for handwriting and simple arithmetic. It looked as though the Admiral planned to spend the long polar night improving the minds of his crew, many of whom, Adam guessed, probably could not read or write.

He groaned. 'I thought I'd escaped all that.'

'They call this Great Cabin,' Pipaluk said. 'Are your parents dead, too?'

'My mother is. She died soon after I was born. I don't remember her. I'm not sure about my father.'

As they moved along the central passageway towards the bows, Adam told her about his father.

'Captain McLellan told me not to get my hopes up, but I can't help it.'

She nodded sympathetically.

Adam produced his precious photograph and showed her. She examined it closely and asked several questions about the harpoon and how it was made.

'And do you have a picture of your mother?'

Adam shook his head. He had always wondered why there had not been a single picture of her in Aunt Emily's house and why his father never carried one. Some had been lost at sea, he had said, and others damaged by damp and salt air. Even so, not one picture between the two of them seemed strange.

'This is the officers' wardroom . . . that means the place where they eat and sit.'

'I know,' Adam replied crossly.

'And here is where the Warrant Officers eat . . . and their cabins, here.'

'What did you and your uncle, Ulu what's-his-name, do when you got to England?'

Pipaluk explained that Admiral Burden gave lectures on his Arctic adventures and that she and Ululik were exhibits.

'We put on our furs and Ululik hurled a harpoon at a stuffed seal. And I chewed on a boot of walrus skin, pretending it was frozen stiff and needed softening.'

Adam could see she was puzzled as to why anyone should want to watch so ordinary a task.

Adam said, 'If you took me back to your country and were giving a lecture about your adventures in England, what would you ask me to do?'

Pipaluk chuckled at the idea. 'I think . . . I think eat with those things . . . spoons and forks, instead of using fingers like normal people do.'

'Is your uncle on board, too?'

'No. He died . . . Measles. I got it too.'

In the forward part of the lower deck they came to an open space where the crew ate and slept. The deck above allowed for seven feet of headroom, but this had been reduced to less than six feet by all the things stowed overhead – the spare planking and spars, the hammocks, and the mess tables, their legs folded, raised on pulleys. A strong animal smell filled the air and Adam could see that beyond the crew's quarters were pens which held two cows. The place was empty. Adam supposed the crew were either working in other parts of the ship or on shore leave. He could see the hooks in the side-beams, no more than fourteen inches apart, from which the hammocks would be slung. In the middle of this space was a boxed-off area in which stood an immense black iron stove. This was the galley where the meals for the entire ship's company were cooked.

Adam looked around. 'So where do I sling my hammock . . . when I get one, that is?'

Pipaluk pointed towards the animal pens.

'Not there! You're joking!'

'No. Not joking. And, look, you could put your hammock just here, near mine.'

Adam wrinkled his nose at the smell.

'You will get used to it,' Pipaluk said. 'You get used to almost anything in time. Look at me. When I came to your land, everything was so strange, so different, at first.'

'Maybe,' Adam muttered, unconvinced.

'That's Milly and that's Daisy,' she said, pointing at the cows.

Smiling happily, she produced, from a pouch in her shirt, a largish bone glistening with lumps of raw meat and offered it to Adam.

'N-n-no thanks.'

She tore off a piece of fat with her teeth, then cracked the bone in her powerful jaws and began to suck out the marrow, smacking her lips with evident satisfaction. She pointed her raw snack in the direction of a ladderway which disappeared downwards.

'Quartermaster's stores. You'll get a hammock there.'

She led him to the orlop deck and banged on a door. Someone slid back a bolt on the other side and opened it. Adam and Skug caught sight of each other at the same time. Both let out loud groans.

'What the hell are you doing here?' Adam demanded.

Skug said, 'I heard Ferret say they was shy of a boy. Never thought you'd turn up. Didn't reckon you had the bottle for it.' He looked at Pipaluk, still with the bone in her hand, and sniggered. 'You know how to pick 'em all right!'

Adam blushed. 'This is Pipaluk,' he mumbled.

'Yeah, I know. A bleedin' peskymow, a savage.'

He turned and led them through a maze of packing cases to the quartermaster's office – a square roofless hut made of wooden boxes, some with 'cheese', some with 'sugar' stencilled on them.

The quartermaster leant over the counter. 'So, here's the other boy what likes fighting and spoiling stores as belong to Her Majesty. Have you been to the palace and begged her forgiveness?'

Adam hung his head. 'I've come to collect my hammock and my...'

'And your Arctic clothing. I expect you'll destroy them given half a chance.'

'No, sir.'

'Well then, let's have a look at you for size.'

The quartermaster sucked air through his teeth. 'Swipe me! We don't stock tackle for tadpoles. You'll just have to make do with what we've got.'

He sent Skug to various corners of the orlop deck to fetch out the items Adam would need.

'Stuff 'em with straw,' the quartermaster said, handing Adam a pair of knee-length boots, three sizes too big.

'Roll 'em up, cut 'em down, pinch 'em in,' he said of the thick serge trousers.

'He won't look exactly nib-like and splash in those, will he?' Skug guffawed.

The quartermaster threw a sausage-shaped bundle at Adam. 'And don't forget your hammock.'

'You'd get three of him in there,' Skug laughed.

'And your seachest for all your gubbins and giggamabobs.'

'Oh, I thought that was his cabin you was giving him!' Skug jeered.

Scowling and biting his lip, Adam packed his chest, tried to heave it onto his shoulder and failed.

'I don't need your help!' he hissed furiously at Pipaluk as she moved to assist him. Carrying the chest awkwardly in front of him, he staggered down the narrow passageway.

'The other way,' Pipaluk whispered.

Adam had to turn and pass Skug again, running the gauntlet of taunts.

'Watch out your girlfriend don't eat you!'

Adam slammed his seachest down on Skug's foot. Skug hopped about howling in pain, then punched Adam in the chest, knocking him to the ground. The quartermaster sprang between them.

'Swipe me if we haven't got a couple of little bantams here! Kill each other for all I care, just don't do it on my territory.'

'Any place suits me,' Skug snarled, nursing his foot. 'I'm going to smash you to pulp, that's what I'm going to do. And when you beg for mercy, I'm going to smash you some more.'

'Huh!' Adam retorted. 'You and whose army?' But he knew he was in bad trouble.

Chapter Four

Adam wandered along Victoria Dock. If he had to fight Skug, he was in for a real hiding. A whole voyage with Skug was . . . Ferret plucked at his sleeve.

'Better get yourself to the galley sharpish or Peggy will do his nut.'

'Who?'

'Jake Peglar, the cook.'

'Oh, no!' Adam exclaimed. What with all that business with Skug, he had clean forgotten that he'd been told to report to the galley after being issued with his clothing. The crew were ashore, getting their last taste of civilisation for many a month, but the officers would be gathering in the wardroom for dinner – not the warrant officers and petty officers, of course, just the toffs. The *Prince Consort* was sailing on the evening tide and it would be the last chance the officers had to all dine together before they were in charge of the various watches – the four-hourly shifts worked by the crew round the clock.

Ferret was gazing longingly at a waterfront tattoo parlour.

'They do the best dragon this side of Java and here's me with not two farthings to rub together.'

'Me neither,' Adam said hastily.

Rolling up a sleeve, Ferret revealed a green serpent which writhed and coiled when he clenched and unclenched his fist.

'Got this one in Kowloon,' he informed Adam proudly.

'Where's that?'

'Well, it ain't where the cow jumped over the moon. And this one . . .'

A silver half-crown piece lay on the cobbles. With a cry of joy, Adam bent to pick it up.

'Don't!' shrieked Ferret, hauling him back. 'It's a wrong 'un.'

Adam looked at him blankly.

'Bad luck, or even worse!' Ferret croaked, visibly shaken by the near miss. 'Tails, see. Never, never pick a coin up what's showing its tail.'

'But a half-crown, Ferret! Half a tosheroon! It's a fortune! You're not going to leave it there?'

'Yes,' Ferret said, pulling Adam by the arm. 'The very thing we're going to do. Oh yes, indeed. And don't you go sneaking back for it later. Makes me weak at the knees to think of the evil 'fluence you could of uncorked. And with us about to sail for God-knows-where, too.'

Looking regretfully over his shoulder, Adam was marched back to the *Prince Consort*.

Considering it would have to cater for over sixty officers and crew, the galley was unbelievably small. The black iron range, glowing with hot coals, occupied one end of the cramped space and Peggy's enormous body almost filled the rest. He advanced towards Adam, wobbling like a jelly, his several chins jouncing with each step, his greasy apron riding up and down on his stomach. His florid face, inflamed by the fierce heat from the range, shone with sweat.

Without taking his eyes off Adam, Peggy's pudgy hand went unerringly to the black jar on a shelf.

'Tell him what happens to boys as is late, Ferret.'

'Oh, no, Peggs, not that. He don't deserve that. Not on his first day!'

A large globule of sweat gathered at the end of Peggy's nose. 'Boys as is late,' he said, 'gets a taste of Pegg's Purge.'

The globule dripped from Peggy's nose onto the range, hissing and spitting. Another bead began to form. 'I'll tell you what,' he said. 'We'll let Solomon decide.' His voice took on an altogether kinder, more loving tone. 'Solomon!' he cooed. 'Come to your daddy, Solomon!'

A black cat emerged from under the range, covered in ashes. Here and there its fur was singed a reddish brown. Peggy scooped Solomon into his arms, rubbing his face against its fur so that a powdering of ashes clung to his sweaty cheek. Again, without needing to look, Peggy fetched down two saucers. He displayed their undersides to Adam. One had 'Yes' painted on it and the other had 'No'. He laid them on the counter and poured milk into each.

'Now, Solomon, my pretty one, shall the bad boy taste my lovely potion, or shall he not?'

Solomon jumped off his shoulder onto the counter. It sniffed at one saucer, then the other, considered the matter for a second or two while it scratched itself, then began lapping at the contents of the saucer marked 'Yes'.

'Aha! The wisdom of Solomon!' Peggy wheezed gleefully. He dipped a wooden spoon into the black jar. 'Open wide, boy!'

The worst medicine imaginable, the bitterest of black molasses, burnt bones, rancid fat, castor oil and rotten fish all combined could not have tasted so awful. Adam wanted to spit it out, scrape the back of his tongue and stuff his mouth with bread to take the taste away.

'Get it down, boy, or there's more.'

Adam swallowed. He writhed on the floor, groaning and retching. Peggy laughed. 'I've known a man beg for a flogging rather than face Pegg's Purge.'

'That stuff can raise the dead, so it can,' said Ferret.

A large drop of sweat plopped into the asparagus soup. 'Start cleaning those saucepans,' Peggy ordered. 'And after that there's the spuds to peel.'

Adam sat on a stool in a corner of the galley, peeling the potatoes. The foul taste lingered in his throat and on the back of his tongue. A kettle hummed, a pot bubbled, the joint inside the oven sizzled. The odours of cooking mingled with the stink of Peggy's sweaty body, Solomon's daily addition to the cold ashes and the smell wafting from the nearby animal pen. Ferret was performing some kind of strange dance, prancing about the galley like a demented leprechaun. It wasn't just that he was avoiding being crushed by Peggy, who was gyrating like a hot-air balloon around the galley.

With his foot Peggy slid open a metal door at one end of the range. 'Soup plates!'

Adam tried to lift out the stacked plates and let out a cry of pain. Ferret, engaged in his demented dance and furiously stirring a bowl at one and the same time, gave a cackle of laughter.

'Sleeves!' he advised.

Adam pulled his sleeves down until they covered his hands and, averting his face from the hot blast that billowed forth, slid the plates out. Solomon retired to his place under the range. Ferret ceased his dance.

Peggy held a soup ladle to his fat lips and sucked. He swilled the soup round his mouth, gargled with it and spat it back into the pot.

He rolled his eyes and sighed. 'Perfect!' he announced.

Adam pushed the trolley carrying the silver soup tureen and the stack of plates towards the wardroom where the officers dined. Beside him was Ferret. Both wore smart white jackets and white gloves – officers and gentlemen, Adam had been told, were not served at table with bare hands.

'What was all that about?' Adam wanted to know.

'What was all what about?'

'Back there in the galley... all that capering lark.'

'It's Solomon. He's got to be walking towards me, or I'm jinxed, see.'

Adam confessed he didn't see and learned that if a black cat walks towards you it brings good fortune, but if it walks away it takes the good luck with it. And so Ferret had to continually manoeuvre himself to make sure Solomon was walking towards and not away from him.

'And that's not easy,' Ferret said. 'I got jinxed and unjinxed three times in there.'

The plates, the tureen and the handle of the silver ladle,

Adam noticed, all had the same crest on them.

'His Nibs' family crest,' Ferret said.

'Admiral Burden?'

'The very same. Brought his own silverware with him, and his own dinner set for twenty-four people, and every blinkin' plate with his crest on it, in gold. And he's brought crates and crates of his own wine.'

A rat scuttled across the passageway. Ferret kicked out at it.

'They'll get worse as the months go by,' he prophesied. 'Unlike us, they thrive in the dark. Cold, scurvy, darkness, rats . . . the four curses of the Arctic.'

How many offspring, he asked Adam, would a mating pair of rats produce if they had twenty young twenty times a year and each of these paired up and did the same?

'A lot,' said Adam.

They arrived at a stout oak door. Ferret knocked and opened it for Adam to push the trolley through. The wardroom was long and narrow. Admiral Charles Burden sat at the far end of the polished walnut table in a high-collared blue jacket with two rows of silver buttons down the front, gold epaulettes on each shoulder and a chest full of medals and ribbons.

'Who's on the Admiral's right?' Adam whispered.

'Captain Quisby, ' Ferret replied through the side of his mouth.

Quisby was the ship's captain, in charge of all matters to do with the ship and its crew. Admiral Charles Burden was the overall commander of the expedition, responsible for carrying out orders from the Admiralty to search for Franklin. On the Admiral's left was Elisha McLellan, the only one not in uniform. Seated on either side of the table were the other twelve officers in their smartest dress uniforms and gleaming brass buttons. Behind each of the diners stood his personal servant, a private of the marines in a scarlet coat. Skug and Pipaluk hovered in a corner ready to assist.

The talk at the table was of the sporting guns they had brought with them in case there was a chance to 'bag' a few animals or birds. And there were several digs at Horse about 'rude mechanicals', and people who preferred to inhale coal dust instead of a good fresh wind.

'You can't halt the march of progress,' Horse declared hotly. 'The age of sail is over.'

There was a chorus of dissent. Heads turned towards the Admiral for his verdict.

He dabbed at his lips with a monogrammed damask napkin. 'As you know, gentlemen, their Lordships at the Admiralty, in their infinite wisdom, gave me no option. No other ship but the *Prince Consort* was offered to me.'

He raised a silver spoon to his lips, then lowered it. 'All of us who engage in Arctic exploration are part of a noble tradition with a code of honour, and to resort to new-fangled inventions is a grubby subterfuge.'

Fingers tapped the table in agreement.

'Dashed unsporting!' someone said and there was another burst of tapping.

All eyes were on Quisby, the ship's captain, to see how

he would react.

'We shall see,' he said quietly. 'Time will tell.'

Horse blurted out, 'But, sir, our engine will greatly assist our passage through the ice.'

The Admiral glared at him. 'I am told, Lieutenant Grenier, that you have brought with you a certain article of clothing purchased from a whaler.'

'Yes, sir, a fur coat. I thought it would . . .'

'Some deplorably ragged Eskimo garment, if I am not mistaken.'

'Yes, sir.'

The Admiral's voice was icy. 'Let me make this clear, gentlemen. We will conquer the Arctic as representatives of the world's greatest and most civilised nation. We will not lower ourselves to the level of savages.'

Adam stole a glance at Pipaluk and then at Elisha. Both their expressions were impassive.

'Excellent soup!' someone exclaimed.

There were murmurs of agreement and the conversation changed to the war which had recently ended in the Crimea, and then to a mutiny which had broken out amongst the native troops in India.

'It just shows that natives can't be trusted!'

'Stab you in the back as soon as look at you.'

'If you ask me, the half-castes are the worst.'

Skug dropped a plate. There was a slight pause in the conversation, then someone said he thought Oxford would thrash Cambridge in the 'Varsity cricket match this summer, starting a heated argument.

Back in the galley, several courses later, Adam began to scrape the leftovers from the roast lamb off the plates into the swill bucket.

'It seems they didn't like the fat.'

With a roar of rage, Peggy seized him by the throat. 'Nobody says that word in my galley! Understand?'

Adam did not understand. He couldn't think what he'd said that had turned the cook into a raving maniac. Still gripping him by the throat, Peggy began to shake him. 'Never, ever, use that word!'

Peggy released him. Adam clutched his throat, gasping for air.

'Look lively!' Peggy bellowed. 'Who are we, lowly scum, to keep their lordships waiting?'

Once again, Adam and Ferret wheeled the trolley towards the wardroom. For a second time, Adam asked, 'What was all that about?'

'Fat,' said Ferret. 'He can't abide that word. He takes it personal, very personal.'

'You might have warned me,' Adam growled and Ferret bared his yellow teeth in what might have been amusement. On the trolley were fruit tart, raspberry jelly and raspberry sauce. Adam wondered, nervously, whether 'jelly' was another dangerous word, never to be uttered in Peggy's presence. On the upper deck, overhead, he could hear the crew coming aboard, reporting back on duty. In less than two hours they would be casting off.

Chapter Five

On the quayside a large crowd had gathered to see the *Prince Consort* set off on her maiden voyage. With her halyards festooned with bunting, she slipped her moorings and steamed down the Thames. The ship's Royal Marine band was playing 'Rule Britannia'. The crowd was cheering and waving flags. Fireworks were exploding, filling the night sky with cascades of light. The entire crew, except for those needed to sail the ship, were lined up on the upper deck in their Number One blues. Adam and Pipaluk stood together near the end of the line. She had followed him up from below. He wasn't sure he wanted her tagging along all the time. That business with the bone and raw meat had been embarrassing. And then she had said something about the tall buildings being like auks' nests crowded together on the cliffs, and people had laughed. She grinned at him and, although he had decided he wouldn't encourage her, he found himself grinning back. He looked away. He'd have to tell her he didn't want her following him around all the time. Tonight he'd sling his hammock somewhere else.

'Rule, Britannia! Britannia rule the waves!' sang the crowd, and somewhere on the far shore a gun boomed out a salute and ships all along the river joined in, hooting their steam sirens.

... thou shalt flourish great and free,
The dread envy of them all.
Rule, Britannia! Britannia rule the waves;
Britons never, never, never will be slaves.

Clear of the dock and the crowd, the *Prince Consort* moved into mid-channel and the parade was dismissed.

Adam said, 'What a carry-on! Anyone would think we were going to the moon.'

Ferret came up beside them. 'Not much difference, if you ask me.'

Adam asked, 'Where do you think we'll be this time tomorrow, Ferret?'

He shrugged. 'Well up the east coast, anyway. Then we'll slip past the Orkneys, keep Iceland to the north of us and head west for Greenland and Baffin Bay.'

Adam felt Pipaluk give a shiver of excitement.

Ferret put a tattooed hand on Adam's shoulder. 'But before all that, we have some unfinished business... down below. Those as not's on duty is waiting to see you and Skug settle things fair and square.'

In the sailors' quarters, the men stood in a circle. An ironic cheer went up as Adam entered. Skug was already there, stripped to the waist. Reluctantly, Adam pulled off his shirt. He didn't like people to see his puny body and hairless chest. Skug was smacking a hard fist into his palm and staring at Adam with a gloating expression. Adam thought, As long as I get in one good shot before I go down, I'll be satisfied. Pipaluk ran forward and pulled

Ferret into the middle. Glancing around, she spotted Jake Peglar. Looking puzzled, he allowed himself to be led by the hand into the ring. Pipaluk sprang onto Peggy's back and up onto his shoulders.

'We Inuit play like this,' she declared. 'Adam here, Skug on Ferret.'

'Good idea, Pipa-Squeak!' someone called out. 'Even up the weight a bit!'

'That's the ticket, lass – make it more sporting!'

'No fun betting on it otherwise.'

After a deal of arguing and laughing and shouting, Adam found himself astride Peggy's shoulders, facing Skug who was riding Ferret. The winner would be the first one to unseat the other. Then someone had the idea to blindfold both pairs of horse and rider.

Adam could hear Peggy wheezing and alternately cursing and letting out high-pitched giggles. More by accident than design they collided with their opponents. A shout went up from the onlookers and Adam guessed that Ferret's spindly legs, which had become even more bandy under Skug's weight, must have nearly given way. Something brushed Adam's face. There was a roar of laughter as he lashed out and connected with a coat which someone had dangled in front of him. He could hear Skug's fists thudding into something.

'Take that, you little squirt!' Skug was shouting. 'And that!'

Adam thought, This isn't going to be so bad, after all – just a bit of a lark, really.

Then Skug's arm was round his neck, hauling him backwards. Adam locked his legs together.

'Choking me!' Peggy croaked, prising Adam's legs apart.

Adam crashed to the floor. Ferret collapsed, tossing Skug on top of Adam. Punches smashed into Adam's face and body. He tore off his blindfold to see Skug, fist raised, leering down at him. Adam covered his face with his hands. After a while, the ferocity of Skug's blows slackened. Through his fingers Adam could see Skug looking round, almost as if he wanted someone to stop him. But Nightingale, a sailor nobody crossed if they could help it, shouted, 'Let's see some blood! That's what we're here for!'

'We want blood! We want blood!' chanted Nightingale's cronies.

Pipaluk ran out of the galley. 'Take that, then!' And she flung the contents of a bowl over Nightingale.

Blood-red fluid dripped down his face. His roar of anger turned to surprised delight.

'Tastes good! Tastes of raspberry!'

Skug didn't resist when Adam wriggled free of his grasp and then the pipe was shrilling for all hands on deck.

'Number Ones, parade order!' came the shouted command.

The *Prince Consort* was passing a wooden battleship which was making her way upriver, pulled by a steam tug. In honour of the expedition, which had captured the nation's imagination, the crew of the battleship were also lined up on parade. An assortment of flags ran up their masthead, the meaning of which Adam did not know, but guessed they were some kind of good luck message. The band of the Royal Marines, in their scarlet tunics, launched into 'Heart of Oak'.

From the fighting ship resounded three hearty cheers, then a bend in the river swallowed her.

'Parade, dismiss!'

Horse joined Adam and Pipaluk at the ship's rail.

'Settling in all right, Adam?'

'Yes, thank you, sir.'

Horse nodded in the direction of the departed battleship. 'The last of her kind. I hear they've begun building an iron battleship. And she'll be steam-driven of course. Times are changing, Adam.' He gave a bitter laugh. 'Even though most of the wardroom won't admit it.'

Adam knew Horse wouldn't have made that remark to anyone else in the crew. Officers were meant to show a united front to the men they commanded. A cabin boy, though, hardly counted as one of the men. He realised, too, that Horse was actually closer in age to himself than he was to most of his fellow officers who had been picked for their long years of Arctic service. However, a ship with engines had to have at least one officer with some knowledge of engineering.

As the river estuary opened out, the ship swayed gently to the motion of the waves. Horse's long face began to turn green. He cast a half-ashamed glance towards Adam and Pipaluk.

'I think I'll trot off and lie down.' He gave an apologetic laugh. 'It still takes me a couple of days to get used to it.'

Adam was dreaming again about the bear. This time it caught him and dealt him a painful blow with its powerful paw. He woke to find Skug's face level with his.

'Like a taste of salt eel, then, would you?' Skug said, referring to the stiff knotted rope's end in his hand, and he whacked the underside of Adam's hammock with it.

'Ow! Clear off!'

'Pipe down over there!' a voice growled.

Skug melted into the shadows.

Adam eased round in his hammock and rubbed his back. The 'salt eel' had been hard. He lay listening to the sounds of thirty or more men asleep. From the darkness a man cried out, another moaned and jabbered something. Feet pattered on the deck overhead. The cattle close by munched and snorted. The smell of hay made Adam remember his father telling him that he hadn't seen an English summer since he was fifteen. He'd always been at the whaling. 'I can no longer recall the smell of new-mown hay, or the sound of a tree in full leaf.' The bear in his dreams was always a creamy white, the same colour as the bearskin rug in Aunt Emily's parlour. His father used to drape it round himself and chase him all over the house, growling fiercely, until Aunt Emily ordered him to stop, saying, 'Can't you see you're terrifying the poor boy?'

He realised that he hadn't, after all, moved his hammock away from Pipaluk. He'd been too tired to find another space in the crowded quarters. Besides, but for her, the fight with Skug could have been a lot worse. He'd have to drop her, though, if he wanted to be seen as one of the men.

Chapter Six

In the galley, the tea in the huge, rectangular copper urn slopped from end to end as the *Prince Consort* lurched and plunged. The mid-afternoon tea and hardtack for the seamen was part of an unvarying routine. Every day for the last three weeks, breakfast had been followed by the daily inspection and then deck scrubbing. At noon the rum ration was issued, accompanied by lemon juice to prevent scurvy. This was followed by more working parties until supper. For those on watch, there was the constant work aloft, altering the sails under the keen eye of the boatswain.

Ferret was performing his usual dance around Solomon, the cat. Adam could see he was jittery about something – even more jittery than usual. Peggy threw three empty sacks at Adam. 'Run up and fetch down more hardtack. The lobster's been told.' By which he meant the marine guarding the casks of ship's biscuits would know that Adam wasn't simply trying to steal them. They were kept on the upper deck where there was a bit of spare space.

Adam wondered what his chances were of running into Skug. He knew Skug's tasks and routine almost as well as he knew his own. That way, he could make sure their paths didn't cross. He would take long, complicated routes from one part of the ship to another to avoid him. A safe place from Skug was in the rigging. Adam knew Skug would never follow him up there. Even so, he'd been given a black eye last week.

Adam emerged onto the upper deck, blinking in the sunlight after the gloom below. He let out a cry of amazement. Icebergs, like sparkling cathedrals, were sailing past. Behind them were the snow-capped peaks of southern Greenland. Adam stared in disbelief at the icebergs, at their miracles of geometry, their fluted cliffs and winged forms. Some radiated sapphire blue, others slid almost imperceptibly from a white so sharp it hurt the eyes to the deep, deep blueness in the caves along their waterline.

'Wow!' breathed Adam.

'My sentiments exactly,' said Horse, appearing from the quarterdeck, a brass sextant in his hand. 'They remind me of the Crystal Palace. Did you ever visit the Great Exhibition?'

'No, sir.'

'Magnificent feat of engineering, more impressive than anything in it, I thought.'

'What's our latitude now, sir?'

'Sixty-six degrees and five minutes North. We'll probably cross the Arctic Circle sometime tomorrow.'

Skug was hurrying along the deck with a note in his hand.

'For me?' enquired Horse.

'No, sir.'

Horse smiled at Skug. 'You can't be a cabin boy forever. Have you thought about what you want to do next?'

Skug shuffled his feet uneasily. 'Er . . . No, not really, sir.'

'You might consider engineering. I'm sure you're clever enough.'

Briefly, Skug's mask of cynical indifference lifted. 'Me?'

'Yes. Well . . . er . . . Carry on, you two.' And Horse disappeared down the companionway.

'So, who is your note for?' Adam asked, hoping to find some neutral topic that wouldn't give Skug a chance to sneer at him.

Skug let out a derisive laugh. 'Was you born yesterday, or what? It's not for anyone. It's just a skive. You carries a note about to look busy, see, so as nobody nabs you for a job.'

Adam blushed. He tried to think of something else to say.

'Bit of a scrowdge down below, isn't it?' It was a word he'd picked up from Ferret, a cross between squeeze and crowd.

'Too right,' Skug agreed.

'At least the orphanage sort of prepared you for it.' Adam knew he'd said the wrong thing as soon as the words were out of his mouth.

Skug's face darkened. His fists clenched. They heard an officer's footsteps approaching. Officers walked in a different way from ordinary folk, with a kind of measured, stately tread. They shot off in different directions, Skug for'ard, Adam aft towards the biscuit casks.

Adam nodded at the marine and flapped the sacks. 'Peggy,' he said.

He examined the herrings which were on top of each cask. They were there to draw the maggots out of the biscuits, since the maggots much preferred to feast on fish. Adam knew for a fact that the biscuits were months old when they were taken on board, despite being sold by his uncle as 'freshly baked this week'. The added weeks at sea were quite long enough for the maggots and weevils in them to multiply in their millions. Every second day, Adam replaced the maggoty herrings with new ones. He found a barrel whose herring had drawn hardly any maggots, which meant the biscuits were ready for use, and filled the three big sacks. As well as being dunked in the tea, the large round biscuits would be hammered into pieces and boiled up with salted codfish to make Poor John for supper. On other days the hardtack was soaked in hot cocoa, or powdered to become dandyfunk, or turned into 'dogs' vomit' by mixing it with oatmeal.

A howl of rage from Peggy greeted Adam on his return.

'Did I say take all day about it? Boys as idles and lazes about instead of doing what they're told gets a taste of you know what.'

'Oh, no, please! Couldn't you at least give me a chance and ask Solomon to decide?'

Peggy regarded him narrowly, but Solomon seemed to know what was going on and was already purring loudly, waiting for the two saucers of milk to be put down. Peggy was powerless to resist the head rubbing against his shins. Quivering and wobbling with emotion, he sighed. 'All right then. But a double dose if Solomon says you're for it.'

Pipaluk was lowering the mess tables by their pulleys. Adam caught her eye and winked.

Thanks to Horse's Inuit coat, Adam had not been made to taste the awful concoction in the jar again. The coat was made from half-cured caribou hide which gave off a powerful smell. Although Horse kept it well wrapped, the enticing odour had not escaped Solomon's notice. He would sit outside Horse's cabin meowing loudly. While making the bed in the cabin, Pipaluk had managed to trim a small piece off the coat and give it to Adam. Every day, when Jake was not in the galley, Adam would take Solomon's saucer, the one with 'No' painted on the bottom, and rub it with the strip of hide. So far, this had not failed him. Four times the bitter question of Pegg's Purge had been put to the judgement of Solomon, and four times Solomon had chosen to drink from the 'No' saucer. It had also resulted in Peggy deciding not to move out of his mother's house when he got back to England, in refusing to lend money to Ferret, and in the crew not getting any spotted dog, their favourite pudding, last Thursday.

'Huh!' Peggy grunted, when Solomon delivered yet another merciful decision.

'What will you do when there's no more milk for him?' Adam asked.

'He'll take a nice fish soup... won't you, my luvlly-wuvlly?'

Adam described the scene up above.

'Huh!' was Peggy's predictable response. He had not left the lower deck since the voyage began. The galley was his kingdom, where he reigned supreme, and he was not interested in anything else.

'Sextant?' Ferret squeaked nervously. 'Did he say what our latitude was?'

Adam paused in his work of pouring tea into mugs and tried to think what Horse had said.

'Yes, it was sixty-six degrees, five minutes North.'

Ferret let out a yell of terror and dived under the table into the huge cauldron used for making porridge for sixty people. His hand appeared, groped for the lid and pulled it in place.

Peggy rolled his eyes heavenwards. 'Friggin' Apocalyptic number. It's the same every time.'

'What's that?'

'The number of the Beast,' moaned the cauldron. 'Six-six-six, and I'm not coming out till you've lit the jinx-removing candles.'

'Top left,' said Peggy. There was a weary resignation in his voice like he'd seen it all before.

Adam fetched the candles down. They were black and fashioned in the shape of occult symbols. Following the instructions issuing from the cauldron, he placed them in a circle round the galley and lit them. They gave off a strong smell of incense.

'Tenshun!' Peggy barked.

He and Adam snapped to attention as Captain Quisby hove into sight. Even Solomon sat up straight.

'At ease!' Quisby snapped. He had a rolled-up chart in his hand. 'That smells good. What's cooking?'

'Oh . . . er . . . special herbs in the stew, sir,' Peggy replied.

'Keeping everything clean and spotless, I see. A place for everything and everything in its place.'

'Yes, Captain.'

'Subdue dirt and disorder wherever they occur.' He tapped his chart. 'Can't abide a blank map. Everything labelled, named, marked down in its proper place, that's how I like it.'

'Yes, Captain.'

Quisby tapped the cauldron with his foot. 'And you scour this thoroughly every day? Not a speck of dirt or a foreign body in it?'

Peggy seemed shocked at the very idea. 'Yes, sir! I mean, no, sir!'

'Hmmm . . . What's for supper tonight?'

'Roast beef for the officers, sir.'

Milly the cow had already been slaughtered and butchered, and Daisy would go the same way when the hay and turnips ran out, which would be soon. Milly had been divided up according to strict protocol. The commissioned officers were allocated the best parts, suitable for roasting or grilling; to the warrant officers and petty officers went the cuts suitable for pot roasting and braising; and the marines and able seamen got the bits only good enough for stewing, boiling and making into pies and puddings.

When Quisby had gone, a frightened Ferret crawled out. 'I'll be all right if I keep inside the Protected Circle, won't I, Peggs?'

'Yes, yes, just get on with the tea. We're behindhand as it is.'

A pipe shrilled. From all directions, men poured into the galley area for their tea break.

Adam was relieved that Peggy kept him far too busy filling mugs to have time to sit with the men while he had his own tea. He felt awkward and embarrassed sitting with the grown men. He didn't know how to respond to their cheery banter and he was sure they were staring at his spots and boils. If they spoke to him as if he was a child, he felt insulted; and when they treated him as an equal, he was floundering, not always understanding what they meant and knowing that any reply sounded ridiculous in a voice that squeaked and piped and growled all in one sentence. He would store up things to say, so as not to sit there completely dumb, but the right moment to say them never seemed to come up.

Peggy bellowed and slapped his own cheek, setting multiple chins in motion. 'Blow me down if we aren't out of apples for their lordships' dinner table. Get yourself down to the hold, lad, and fetch up a sackful.'

Adam arrived at the bottom of the ladder. Raising his lantern aloft he moved slowly past the square, iron water tanks, trying not to breathe in the reek of sewage, coal dust and fumes. Rats scuttled in the dark. Behind him, he could hear the boiler wheezing and stokers shovelling coal. Although the engines were idle to save coal for when they would be needed to force a way through the ice, the lower deck had to be heated by overhead pipes. He walked along the wooden duckboards below which the foul, oily bilge water darkly heaved and slapped. He wondered if anything lurked in its depths. Adam found the stacks of slatted boxes containing the apples and filled his sack. Out of nowhere Skug landed on his back, knocking him flat. Pinning Adam with his knee, Skug prised up a square of duckboard. He forced Adam's head through the gap towards the stinking, slopping bilge.

'So, you think you're better than an orphan boy, do you?'

'I never said that!'

'It's what you meant. You think, 'cos I got no mother and father, I'm dirt.'

Adam strained to keep his face clear of the bilge. Coughing and choking from the foul vapours, he gasped out, 'I don't, Skug, I don't! I don't have a mother, either, and maybe not a . . .'

For a fraction of a second Skug loosened his grip. With all his strength Adam twisted round and pushed him away. Seizing his sack and his lantern, he raced into the labyrinth of narrow passages between the stacks of crates. Between the iron water tanks and the deck above was a small gap. He blew out the candle in his lantern and attached it and the sack to his belt before climbing up and squeezing into the space. He could hear Skug searching for him, coming nearer.

Skug stopped directly beside the water tank. He was

breathing hard in a harsh, uncontrolled way. He banged the flat of his hand hard against the side of the tank, again and again. The sound boomed and reverberated through the darkness. And then another sound reached Adam's ears . . . Skug was crying.

The cold pierced Adam's clothes, his flesh, his bones, but he went on lying there, even though Skug had moved on. He'd be in trouble with Peggy when he got back to the galley, but that didn't seem to matter. He was confused. Skug was the causer of pain and misery, not someone who felt these things. He didn't want his hatred of Skug weakened by pity. Skug was the enemy and, if you went soft on your enemy, you were sunk. And what about those things he had found himself blurting out? 'I don't have a mother,' he had panted. The fact was he didn't remember her. There was not a single photograph or picture of her and Aunt Emily was always so evasive when he asked about her. 'And don't go pestering your father about it. It will only make him sad, and you don't want that, do you?' It struck Adam like a physical blow, so that he nearly cried out. He didn't know his own mother's name! How could he not have realised that before? He had always thought of her as 'Mother'. And then, that other thing he had blurted out to Skug. 'Maybe I don't have a father,' he had nearly said. Had he simply said it in the hope that Skug would let him go, or was that what he really believed? Deep down, did he know his father was dead, and was simply refusing to face up to it?

Chapter Seven

In Great Cabin, Adam sat at a table with Pipaluk beside him. You had to get permission to use the ship's library or to study in Great Cabin. Luckily, Horse was the one you had to ask and he was full of encouragement for Adam's efforts to teach Pipaluk to read and write and of hers to teach Adam the rudiments of Kalaallisut, the language of the Greenland Inuit. Great Cabin was also a good place to keep out of Skug's way, although they didn't tell Horse that. Earlier this morning, Skug had tried to enlist Adam in a game he liked to play. It consisted of innocently engaging the good-natured Horse in conversation and seeing how many words associated with horses you could get him to say. 'Nay, lad,' was almost too easy, and, since Horse was mad about engines, so was 'horsepower'. Questions about the rolling motion of the ship might get you 'stable' and so on. Of course, Skug needed an audience to show off to, someone to keep the score and admire his horsemanship. It had been tempting to be on the same side as Skug for once, doing the baiting instead of being baited. But Adam liked Horse and it would have been a kind of betrayal. He had walked away. Skug wouldn't forget that.

Pipaluk got up and opened the big chest in the corner – the dressing-up chest. It was intended for 'theatricals' and other entertainments to help pass the long winter night which would descend on them in November. In

May the pack ice, the large slabs of frozen sea ice which clogged Davis Strait, usually began to break up. Even so, it might take three weeks or more to butt their way through the ice until they came to the wider, comparatively ice-free waters of Baffin Bay. This would give them a little over two months, perhaps until mid-August, before the sea began to freeze over. They would then be trapped in the ice until next spring, when the search for Franklin would resume.

Laughing, Pipaluk tried on a flowery ladies' hat. Adam found a cocked hat rather like the one Admiral Burden wore.

'Bumble!' he crowed, assuming a portly swagger.

The nickname had spread through the ship within hours of being invented. Charles Burden or CB had turned into Sea Bee, then Bumble Bee and finally, Bumble.

The door opened and Elisha McLellan entered.

'Do you two have permission to be in here?'

'Yes, Captain McLellan,' Adam answered.

Elisha's expression became a fraction less stern. 'Everything going all right, Adam?'

'Yes, thank you.'

'It may not seem like it, Adam, but I am watching out for you, as your father would have wanted... Only, as I'm sure you are aware, if the men thought I was favouring you, they'd give you a hard time.'

'I know... Pipaluk, here, is teaching me Kalaallisut.'

Elisha smiled. 'I hope she has taught you the most useful word of all – "imaaqa."'

'What's that?'

'It means "maybe". Nothing is ever certain in the Arctic – the weather, the amount of ice, the ways of the whales.'

He paused and took out his pipe and began to fill it. Pipaluk pulled her own clay pipe from her pocket and held it out to be filled.

'Pipaluk!' Adam hissed, trying to warn her it was not good manners to ask for things.

Chuckling, Elisha gave her a fill. 'Different people, different customs, Adam.'

Adam asked, 'How long will it be before Pipaluk reaches her home? Bumb...er...I mean, the Admiral did promise...'

'It's at least another hundred miles up the coast. As I said, maybe that's three days, maybe it's three weeks, maybe not till next year.'

'Where will we be heading after that, Captain? Nobody's told us.'

'Well,' said the Ice Master, frowning, 'Admiral Burden has his own ideas about where we might find any trace of those unfortunate men. He intends to head north.'

'North? But Franklin was heading west, through Lancaster Sound, wasn't he?'

Elisha nodded grimly and Adam could see from the way his jaw clamped on the stem of his pipe that he did not agree with the Admiral.

Up above, commands were being shouted, feet were running.

Elisha glanced upwards. 'They'll be mooring the ship to an iceberg. We must have crossed the line.' He smiled at Adam. 'You'd better get yourself up on deck, ready for the fun.'

'What line?' Pipaluk wanted to know, as they hurried off.

'The Arctic Circle.'

'There isn't a line. We, the Inuit, would know about it if there was.'

'It's not a real line,' Adam explained. 'You can't see it. You just know it's there. At least, the officers say they do.'

'Ah! It must be part of the qallunaat Spirit World. We have a Spirit World, too.'

Everyone was grouped below the foretop. The band struck up. The order was given, 'Hands to dance and skylark!' – the signal for the sailors to start games of leapfrog and tag and to dance to the lively music. And when the band stopped for a rest, the several fiddlers amongst the crew took over, making the decks bounce to the rhythm of stomping feet.

Finally, the long-awaited command was given, 'Splice the main brace!' and an extra ration of rum was issued. Adam was only allowed a half-ration. Like most of the sailors, he drank his with a good quantity of water. But one or two, following Nightingale's lead, tossed it down neat. Skug did the same. Adam saw him turn green and hurry to the rail. Adam followed him. He wasn't quite sure whether he wanted to gloat as Skug vomited over the side, or whether it was because nobody on board gave two hoots for Skug and to have nobody who cared for you was a terrible and frightening thing.

'Push off!' Skug snarled and doubled over the rail, heaving up his guts.

Below decks, Adam saw Pipaluk bending over a bucket. Was she being sick, too? She straightened up and smiled, running her hands through her wet hair.

'But that's urine!' Adam exclaimed, horrified.

Behind him there came a cry of triumph. 'Pippa-piss-pot!' Skug jeered. 'Pippa-piss-pot!'

Adam hurled himself at Skug, uncertain whether it was because of the insult to Pipaluk or to cover his own revulsion at what he'd seen. Skug twisted Adam's arm behind his back.

'Say "Pippa-piss-pot", or I'll break you arm!'

'I won't.'

Skug yanked on his arm. Adam yelped with pain.

'Say it!'

Then it was Skug who was roaring in pain. Pipaluk's teeth were clamped into his calf. He let go of Adam.

'Crazy cannibal! Stupid savage!' He hobbled off, cursing.

'Thanks,' Adam muttered. He couldn't meet her eye, because part of him half agreed with Skug.

That evening, Daisy was butchered – the last of the fresh meat. From now on they'd have nothing but salt horse. In the lower deck the men were quiet and pensive, as if crossing the line meant passing into some new and dangerous realm. Sometime during the night, they said, they were likely to reach the edge of the pack ice. And, in the galley, Ferret lit his jinx-removing candles. He had seen three seagulls flying close together, directly overhead, a warning of death soon to come.

Chapter Eight

In May, this far north, it got light early. Adam's hammock swung in time with the others. The crashing of the reinforced bows against the ice and the thumping pistons of the engines made sleep difficult. For two weeks the *Prince Consort* had been pushing its way through the pack ice which choked Davis Strait. He understood now how his father could have drifted off on an ice floe. Sometimes the slabs of sea ice were jammed together so that you could leave the ship and walk for half a mile or more, jumping from one ice plate to another. Then a change of wind direction, a swell rolling in, or a tidal current would break them up and float them apart. The other day Adam had seen a polar bear lolloping along parallel to the ship, about a quarter of a mile away. The speed with which it could run had filled him with terror. Clearly a polar bear could outrun a man. That night he dreamt again that the bear was stalking him.

Adam reached up and felt his shirt and trousers which were draped around one of the hot pipes. They'd be dry in an hour, he reckoned. Several days ago the water in the iron tanks had frozen, so that fresh water was in short supply. Every few days, a working party would land on an iceberg and chip away ice for melting down into drinking water. There was none to spare for washing clothes – except for the officers, of course. If salt water was used, the clothes never completely dried. So the men collected urine in a tub and used that. Its smell was definitely preferable to the sour, stale odour of dirty clothes. Adam had washed his own things this way only yesterday. He saw now, that when Pipaluk used urine for her hair, it was not some filthy, primitive custom, but the same common sense solution that Arctic sailors had used for centuries when water freezes and fuel is precious.

Later that day, shots rang out from the upper deck. Adam, on a mission to the biscuit barrels with Ferret, saw that the officers with their sporting guns and the marines with their rifles were getting a bit of target practice. A colony of several hundred seals was on a nearby ice floe. The bull seals slithered and flopped to the edge of their floe and disappeared beneath the water, but the pups were still too young to move. Their mothers stayed with them and died in the hail of bullets, the onlookers cheering each hit. The *Prince Consort* ploughed on through the pack ice, leaving behind an ice floe running with blood and littered with bodies.

'Senseless!' Horse exclaimed. He had not been one of the sporting gentry with a gun.

'But there were so many of them!' Ferret exclaimed. 'It's not as if we're ever going to finish them all off.'

He rubbed the stub of his frostbitten nose. 'Seals is always the first to show, then unicorns, then the whales.'

Adam was intrigued. 'Unicorns?'

'Kind of a small whale with a single long horn on its snout.'

'Narwhal,' Elisha McLellan said, joining Horse at the rail. 'Its horn was worth its weight in gold when people thought it came from a unicorn.'

'Look!' Adam exclaimed.

An expanse of open sea appeared to be hovering above the horizon, inverted, with streaky clouds beneath it.

'Cold air causes refraction,' said the Ice Master. 'It's a kind of mirage. What you're seeing could be a long way off, but at least we know there is open water beyond the pack.'

In fact, the *Prince Consort* broke through to the open water the next day. The engines were stopped, the sails piled on and a course set for Greenland's north-west coast. They were aiming for the place where, three years ago, Bumble Burden had taken Pipaluk and her uncle on board. Pipaluk could hardly contain her excitement. Already she was beginning to recognise distant features – the mountain peak with a silhouette like a bear's face, the island humped like a whale.

'I expect the Great Lover will pine away without his girlfriend,' was Skug's latest jibe.

'I will not!'

But Adam knew he would miss her... more than he cared to admit, even to himself. He had tried to cast her in the role of a nuisance, who stuck to him like a limpet, but it wasn't working. Somehow, she had grown on him. They had become a sort of team.

The mirages and optical illusions continued. A stretch of

coastline, about two miles off, multiplied, tier upon tier, to become immense, layered cliffs. A sailing ship was sighted, its topsails impossibly elongated. Then its hull ballooned into grotesque shapes, while the masts and sails divided into a series of separate dwarfish forms.

'Upernaadlit,' Pipaluk said to Adam.

'What's that mean?'

'Those who come in spring. The whalers.'

The word soon ran round the *Prince Consort* that it was the *Resolution,* one of the Hull whaling fleet. She was on a north-westerly course, probably making for the whaling grounds off Baffin Island.

A cry came from the crow's nest. 'Small boat on starboard bow!'

Pipaluk seemed to know. She ran to the starboard rail, pointing to where her keen eyes had picked out a tiny craft bobbing in the waves. Sometimes it disappeared altogether, sometimes just the flashing blade of a double-ended paddle could be seen, then it would ride up on a crest to reveal a man in a narrow boat made of skins approaching on a course to intercept the *Prince Consort.*

'Qortoq!' Pipaluk screamed with delight. 'It's my other uncle – Ululik's brother, Qortoq!'

Qortoq manoeuvred his kayak alongside the ship. Adam had never seen an Inuit kayak before. It was about fifteen feet long and hardly wider than Qortoq's hips. He wore a sealskin jacket the bottom end of which was fastened round the rim of the cockpit, making the craft watertight. Qortoq grasped the rope which had been lowered to him and was hauled up to deck level, still sitting in his kayak. He unfastened the apron of his jacket and climbed out, beaming all over his face. He was short and thickset, with straight grizzled hair and a face like a walnut. He wore bearskin trousers and sealskin boots like Pipaluk. She ran forward into his outstretched arms. They hugged and laughed and talked nineteen to the dozen, and hugged and laughed some more, until the boatswain coughed and said to Pipaluk that Captain Quisby wanted to know who their unexpected visitor was.

'My uncle, Qortoq, is a highly respected angakok.'

'What's that when it's at home?' the boatswain wanted to know.

Pipaluk consulted Adam.

'A shaman,' Adam said.

'I'm none the wiser,' said the boatswain.

'A kind of wizard,' Adam replied.

'A healer,' Pipaluk added. 'A person who sees into the future and talks to the gods.'

'Jesus!' said the boatswain.

Qortoq had seen in a trance that his Pipaluk was aboard the white man's big boat. He had paddled for twenty-three days, stopping only occasionally for short rests, in order to greet his niece and accompany her back to their settlement. At this point, Qortoq said something to Pipaluk, tapping the skin bag he had pulled from the interior of the kayak.

'He says to tell you he has also brought a few useless

bits and pieces which nobody would really want. He foolishly hopes to trade them for the wonderful things the gods have given the white men who deserve them so much more than the unworthy Inuit.'

Behind Adam, Elisha chuckled softly. 'Don't be fooled by all that modesty,' he said in Adam's ear. 'It's just their way.'

While this translation was taking place, Qortoq helped himself to a herring on the top of a biscuit barrel, his tongue darting around his lips to capture any escaping lice.

'There's a sack of coals heaping up, and no mistake,' remarked a sailor, glancing skywards. 'We're in for a sneezer.'

Captain Quisby, too, had read the signs of a coming storm. He gave the order to reduce canvas. Under the boatswain's direction, sailors swarmed up the rigging, furling the topsails and reefing in the mainsail. They worked fast, knowing that storms in the Arctic could come out of the blue with a suddenness and a ferocity that was hard to believe.

Within minutes the southeasterly gale fell shrieking upon them, whipping the sea into a frothing cauldron, filling the air with spume. The *Prince Consort* heeled over, then changed course and fled before the storm, speeding westwards further and further away from the Greenland coast and everything dear to Pipaluk.

The lower deck was crowded. The usual working parties had been cancelled. Above, waves were breaking over the ship and sluicing along the decks. A seaman, Pedro Lee, had been washed overboard while trying to batten down a loose hatch. Those on watch were waiting below, dressed in their oilskins, ready to be called out if necessary. Most of the others had taken to their hammocks. The ship was pitching to and fro so violently that this was the best place to be. The hammocks swung in unison – towards the stern as the Prince Consort climbed a steep wave, back the other way as it plunged into the abyss. A sailor was moaning in pain, clutching a crushed finger. Every time the hatch opened to let somebody in or out, there was a volley of curses as torrents of sea water cascaded in.

'It's a wonder Quisby's not got us scrubbing the decks!' Nightingale called out and won a laugh.

Adam, with Ferret beside him, was in the galley, mop in hand, trying to repel the rivers of water which rushed towards the galley with each tilt of the deck. Anything which got past the mops hit the big iron stove and went up in hissing clouds of steam. Adam was having difficulty keeping on his feet, even with the mop as a third leg. The noise was incredible. Every timber in the ship seemed on the move, adjusting to the strain, groaning under the pressure. Loose seachests slid up and down. And each time the *Prince Consort* hit a trough it was as though it had run into a solid wall.

'The *Prince* is in good voice today,' Ferret observed.

'Every ship sounds different.'

'Are we going to sink, Ferret?'

'Not a chance. Don't have Peggy's permission, see. Isn't that right, Peggs?'

Peggy, with Solomon perched on his shoulders, was fixing up gimbals from which to hang his pots. These rods and bearings rotated with the motion of the ship and ensured that the pot was always horizontal no matter how rough the sea was.

He boasted to Adam, 'I've never failed to produce a hot meal on time yet, not in twenty years. Hurricanes, pirates, mutiny – nothing's stopped me and I don't aim to spoil that record now.'

Crash! The whole ship shuddered as a giant wave swept over it. Adam could hear it swooshing along the deck overhead, exploding against things.

'Don't just stand there like a hypnotised rabbit, boy! Help Ferret lift that cauldron of soup up here.'

'Thick pea soup,' said Ferret, bouncing off Peggy's stomach. 'My favourite.'

A cupboard door flew open. A bar of soap shot out, straight into the soup. Another surge of water hit the stove, hissing and spitting.

'Keep the fire going, boy! Fish that soap out! Keep mopping! Ferret, the soup needs salt in it.'

Bang! Adam was thrown to the floor with the violence of the impact. Water was jetting through the cracked and splintered hull, spraying the galley.

'We hit ice!' the boatswain shouted. 'Watch on deck!'

There was a scramble up the companionway. The men would be fighting to lower canvas pads over the damaged part. Meanwhile the carpenter and his team were trying to board up the hole from inside.

'Won't need it now,' Ferret said.

'What?'

'Salt . . . in the soup. Took a right good dose of the briny just then.'

Peggy hauled Adam to his feet and thrust a wooden spoon into his hand. 'Never mind what's going on over there. Nothing can be worse than doing without good hot grub when you need it. So get stirring!'

Chapter Nine

Outside the protection of the bay the wind was stampeding white horses across the ice-flecked sea. For five days the damaged *Prince Consort* had run before the storm. On reaching the coast of Baffin Island, Captain Quisby had brought her into a safe haven. As well as the holed hull, the vat of lemon juice in the hold had broken loose and been smashed to pieces.

'Must be the nicest smelling bilge a ship ever had,' Ferret said.

'And rats with the sourest faces,' Adam replied.

But the surgeon was not amused. Without the daily ration of lemon juice, the crew were threatened with scurvy.

Sheltering in the natural harbour, too, were four whaling ships from Hull – which was why Adam was in the galley helping prepare a special dinner. Captain Quisby had invited the captains of the whaling fleet and the two wives who had accompanied their husbands to come aboard later that evening.

'Will those potatoes be long, Adam?' Peggy asked, while doing three things at once.

'No, I think they'll be round,' Adam answered. It just slipped out because his mind was elsewhere. He knew he was going to regret it. At least Solomon's saucer was properly primed with a good smearing of Horse's coat. In case the strip of hide lost its potency, Pipaluk had taken fresh cuttings on several occasions. Yes, he should be all right there. But Peggy could fly into a raving paddy-whack at the drop of a saucepan and that was no joke when the place was full of sharp knives, cleavers, rolling pins and any number of things to hurl about.

Adam's mind had been on his father. Would any of the whalers have known him and would they be able to tell him anything new about what had happened to him? His father had been with the Whitby fleet and these were Hull men, but most whalers had crossed paths at one time or another.

Luckily, Peggy was distracted by Pipaluk's arrival. 'Captain Quisby's compliments, Mister Peglar, and can he please have some of your excellent hot chocolate brought to Great Cabin as soon as possible.'

'How many?' Peggy sighed.

'For three.'

Pipaluk turned to go.

'Hold on, girl! Wait here and take it yourself.'

'I am needed,' she said, 'to speak for Qortoq . . . to . . . to . . .'

'Interpret,' Adam said.

She threw him a grateful glance.

Peggy wobbled with rage. 'Damn them to Hell! How am I supposed to turn out two hundred meals a day and do special occasions and God knows what else if they keep stealing my kitchen hands?' He waved Pipaluk away. 'Go, if you must!' He glared at Adam. 'I suppose you'll have to take it, then.'

In Great Cabin Qortoq was peering with pretended dismay into his bag. Captain Quisby and Elisha McLellan sat watching him. Adam put down the tray with the jug of hot chocolate and the cups.

Elisha said, 'Permission for the boy to stay, sir. He might learn something.'

Quisby nodded. 'Try and be quick with this Eskimo fellow, Captain McLellan. I have things to do before this tedious dinner party begins.'

Elisha gave Quisby a hard stare, but said nothing. He knew very well that Quisby regarded whalers as boring, uneducated people with no refined or uplifting conversation worth gracing a civilised dinner table. Only Quisby's belief in strict adherence to the code of naval etiquette had made him invite them.

Elisha turned to Qortoq. 'We would like to see fox skins,' he said, and Pipaluk translated.

Through his niece, Qortoq replied, 'It happens that a very poor hunter is present. There are no fox skins in my bag. It takes a skilled hunter to catch a fox.'

'I am desolate,' said Elisha, who knew the way these things should be done. 'What is it you have in your bag?'

'Nothing to be spoken of in this splendid company.'

'I hoped they were fox skins.'

Qortoq doubled up with mirth. 'I have nothing but old scraps of fur used for wiping my hands and swabbing the greasy floor.'

'Suppose you let me look at them. I have waited a long time to see some really fine fur.'

'I would be ashamed to let you see them. I meant to throw them away, but forgot, being a foolish, ignorant person.'

The exchange continued in this way for some time until Qortoq finally pulled out three magnificent furs and the real bargaining began. Quisby had brought with him on the expedition his own supply of tobacco, tea, needles, knives and harpoon heads for this very purpose. It was one of the perks of being captain that he could add quite a bit to his pay by trading for furs which would sell for a high price in England. To Adam's amazement Qortoq insisted that, in return for a knife, he should give even more fox pelts than Quisby wanted.

'I will be more pleased with my knife if I pay five pelts, not three. Then I will know it is good and everyone will admire it.'

'Savages are like children,' Quisby remarked, staring with an expression of amused superiority at Qortoq. 'Treat them like children and you won't go far wrong.'

Pipaluk flushed and bit her lip.

Elisha said quietly, 'Without respect for people you can go very far wrong.'

The dinner party was in full swing. At the far end of the wardroom the band of the Royal Marines was playing a medley of waltzes. In addition to Captain Quisby and the six guests from the whaling ships, Elisha was also at the table. Adam had taken Ferret's place as steward because of what had happened during the fish course. Ferret had returned to the galley from the wardroom ashen-faced and gibbering. Arctic trout had been served, caught that morning in the stream that flowed into their sheltered bay. Instead of eating his fish from head to tail, Quisby had started at the wrong end, thereby going from good luck to bad luck.

'He's the cap'n, isn't he?' croaked Ferret. 'He stands for all of us on this doomed voyage.' And, clutching a jinx-removing candle, he had curled up inside the porridge pot and refused to come out.

Mrs Parker, the wife of the *Hebe's* captain, looked up as Adam's white-gloved hands slid a dirty plate out of the way. 'You're Nathaniel Jones's boy, aren't you? I heard you were aboard.'

'Yes, ma'am.'

'We were all sorry to hear about your father.'

Panic rose inside Adam. She was talking as if he was definitely dead.

She was saying, 'He had quite a reputation, your father.'

Adam started to flush with pleasure, but she tapped him on the chest and said severely, 'I hope you're not going to take after...'

Elisha coughed loudly.

Mrs Parker covered her mouth with her napkin. 'I... er... I mean a career in the Royal Navy is so much more respectable, isn't it, Captain Quisby?' Her tone had a sharp edge.

Quisby inclined his head ever so slightly in

acknowledgement of the remark.

Captain Bruce of the *Resolution* said, 'Nathaniel was one of the best spectioneers in the business, one of the very best, until—'

'So, what was last year's catch like?' Elisha cut in.

Captain Bruce replied, 'Last year the *Resolution* took close on seventeen thousand seals and four whales. But that was fewer than in '56 and even less than '55 and this year all the signs are that our catch will be even smaller.'

Elisha put his elbows on the table and leant across to Captain Bruce. Then, remembering he was not at home on his own whaler, but in the officers' wardroom of one of Her Majesty's ships, he hastily withdrew them. 'We can't go on taking such large numbers for ever.'

Parker took his eye off the peas on his fork. 'I don't see why not. The ocean's vast. There will always be plenty of whales. It's just a matter of finding them.'

His wife surreptitiously fielded the peas which had rolled across the white damask tablecloth.

'Aye,' agreed Bruce. 'Reckon they've got a sight more cunning these days. But they're there all right... somewhere.'

Adam arrived back in the galley, carrying a stack of dirty plates, his mind on what Mrs Parker had said. What could she have meant? Peggy was screeching with rage and, for once, Adam was not the cause of it. Qortoq was rubbing his stomach and licking his lips while peering into all the cupboards, oblivious to Peggy's threats and near apoplexy. He paused for a long time over the figure curled up in the large pot, casting several curious and uneasy glances at Peggy. Then he spotted Solomon, smiled broadly and made approving noises. His good humour restored by having his beloved pet admired, Peggy lifted Solomon and offered him to Qortoq to stroke. Qortoq took Solomon, drew his newly-acquired knife and was about to cut the cat's throat when Peggy let out a high-pitched scream and hit Qortoq on the head with a wooden spoon. Using his immense weight, he pushed Qortoq up against the sink, reached for Pegg's Purge and forced some between the bewildered Inuit's teeth. A blissful smile slowly spread over Qortoq's face. He smacked his lips and opened his mouth wide for more.

'What do you want for that ring on your finger?' the porridge pot asked Qortoq.

After a bit of haggling, an ivory ring carved with weird symbols was exchanged for a jinx-removing candle. Qortoq promptly ate the candle and Ferret put on the ring, declaring that a ring straight from a wizard's finger must be unique and bound to bring good luck. Adam didn't tell Ferret that he had seen two more exactly like it when Qortoq had laid out his wares in Great Cabin.

Adam tried to remove the empty pudding plates as discreetly as possible. The whalers around the table were reminiscing about the great disaster of 1830. Out of the ninety-one ships in Baffin Bay that year, nineteen were lost and ten seriously damaged, all crushed by the ice. There had been an unusual amount of ice in the spring of that year which never dispersed. Winter had come early and severe storms had driven the ice into compact, crushing masses.

Captain Bruce who, as a young man, had been on one of the stricken ships, said, 'In all my years in the Arctic, I've never seen anything like it.' He turned to Elisha. 'You were there. What about you?'

The Ice Master stared thoughtfully into his brandy glass. 'I'm thinking that, maybe, this year will be its equal. All the early signs seem to suggest it.'

There was a rumble of agreement from the whalers.

Captain McKenzie of the *Hope* refilled his glass from the circulating decanter. 'And there's been reports that, as far south as Pond's Inlet, the winter ice has not even begun to break up yet. I have my doubts about seeing the season out. I've a mind to cut my losses and sail for home.'

Quisby gave a scornful laugh. 'What happened in 1830 was more than a quarter of a century ago. Since then, we have become masters of an empire and masters of Nature.'

Elisha spoke in deadly earnest. 'Do not underestimate the power of the ice. I have never seen so much at this time of year.'

Quisby raised an eyebrow as if in disbelief. 'Look at the *Prince Consort,* gentlemen – modern design, powerful engines, a reinforced hull, all the latest equipment, an elite and well-disciplined body of men – we at least, I assure you, have nothing to fear.'

Chapter Ten

In the stern of one of the *Prince Consort*'s boats the smell of eau de Cologne was overpowering. Adam sat with Pipaluk, Elisha and Horse as eight sailors and petty officers, double-banked with an oar apiece, pulled towards the *Rose*. Although it was seven in the evening, the sun was high in the sky. The Hull fleet was returning hospitality. They had invited the entire crew of the *Prince Consort* to visit them. The four whaling ships would be entertaining a dozen or so men each – which was why the men were 'square-rigged' in their best go-ashores. Quisby and Bumble had declined the invitation, saying they were too busy. And Peggy, of course, refused to leave his galley. He had gone all snifty-snidey about the cooks on the whalers, declaring, 'Those slusheys couldn't cook hot water for a barber!'

To Adam's relief Skug had been assigned to *Hebe*. This morning, Skug had smacked him across the head yet again and called him 'a fat-headed galley-swab'. An idea suddenly came to Adam. He smiled to himself and stored it away for when the moment was right. Then a frown crossed his face. Skug had been given an oar. Skug was rowing alongside the men, not sitting uselessly in the stern like he was.

Beyond the protecting arms of the bay, the gale force wind was gradually dying down. Tomorrow the bay would be empty of ships for, in the short Arctic summer, there was not a day to be wasted. The Hull fleet would weigh anchor and go in search of the whales. The *Prince Consort*, though, would stay behind for at least another day while repairs to the damaged bow were completed. Adam looked inland. Jagged grey-blue ridges bit into a clear blue sky. A part of Adam longed to be up there amongst the glistening snowfields, drinking the champagne air cupped in the high corries.

He sat silent, fingering his spots. He couldn't think what to say to Horse or Elisha. Everything that came to mind seemed like it might sound naïve, or childish or just plain stupid.

Horse said, 'The breeze out there . . . Dying down a bit. The white . . . er . . . thingummies are much smaller now.' He turned to the Ice Master. 'It will be quite like old times for you, Captain McLellan.'

'It will that.'

The four of us sitting here in the stern are a load of misfits, Adam thought. And he himself was the biggest misfit of all. This was a man's world and he was neither boy nor man, but some confusing, half-cocked, pimply, in-between sort of creature.

As they neared the *Rose,* the sweet, heavy smell of whale oil and the odour of slobgollion and blubber reached their nostrils. Elisha breathed deeply, savouring the familiar smell. Seabirds wheeled overhead – kittiwakes, mollies, puffins, dovekies and the noisy glaucous gulls, known as burgomasters.

Horse said, 'I wonder what we'll get to eat.' A thought which was not a million miles from Adam's mind.

'Well, it won't be crang, I can tell you that,' Elisha said. Crang, as Adam knew, was whale meat. The whalers never ate it. Once the blubber had been stripped from the carcass, the rest was left to rot. Just occasionally the crang might be boiled down to extract what little oil was in it and then sold as fertiliser or cattle food.

'Kilaluga-hoi!' Pipaluk called out.

Beyond the bay a pod of narwhals, the sea unicorns, were surging through the water, their dappled, grey-green backs occasionally breaking the surface, their long spiral horns jousting with the waves.

Jugged hare was what they got to eat, sitting on benches at long tables on the lower deck. The hares had been snared by some of the crew who had gone ashore. Then came roast dovekies, half a dozen or more of the little plucked birds to a plate. The captain and his mate had been blazing away at them all day. Only the ones that fell on the deck were harvested, but that was plenty enough. The *Rose* was a 'dry' ship, so no alcohol was served. Instead, there was lashings of strong, sweet tea.

'When is a leaky old tub dry?' muttered Bungs, the cooper, who was sitting next to Adam.

'When its captain is a temperance man,' answered Adam, who had heard it before.

On Adam's other side was Tom, the *Rose*'s cabin boy, about a year older than him. Tom told him several lewd jokes which Adam didn't fully understand, but at which he laughed loudly.

A few places away, Elisha was discussing the price of whale oil. Adam remembered his father talking about 'bringing light from the dark depths of the sea', by which he meant that whale oil lit the streetlamps of the nation's towns. Now, most towns used gaslight.

'Not to worry,' said the *Rose*'s first mate. 'This is the machine age and machines need oil and always will.'

'But what about the whales?' Elisha demanded. 'Will there always be enough of them?'

'Of course!' protested the first mate. 'There are so many, how could there ever be not enough? There might be a bad season or two, but . . .'

Bungs was getting annoyed. Some of the whalers were teasing him. All those places that Royal Naval expeditions to the Arctic claimed to have discovered, they said, had been known to whalers for years.

'And, even before that, to us, the Inuit,' said Pipaluk quietly.

They either didn't hear her or chose to ignore her.

'So how come you blubber hunters don't have your names on any maps?' Bungs wanted to know.

''Cos we're up against other fleets. We're all rivals, see? You don't let on if you've found a better route or a good island for shelter, not if you've any sense.'

'Huh!' scoffed Bungs.

'We come here year in year out. Just 'cos we don't give ourselves airs and graces and call ourselves an expedition . . .'

Mrs Worthington, the captain's wife, clapped her hands. 'Now boys! Keep it friendly! I'd say it was time for a sing-song!'

She moved to the organ in the corner which was operated by a foot pump. She was a small, thin woman. To the best of Adam's recollection, she had hardly said a word while on board the *Prince Consort,* but here she was, bursting into song, encouraging everyone to join in.

Our captain stood upon the deck,
A spyglass in his hand,
A-viewing of the Greenland whales
That blowed at every strand.
Get to your boats, my boys
And we'll have a ton of oil!
Be brave, my lads! Let hearts not fail
While the bold harpooner is a-striking of the whale,
While the bold harpooner is a-striking of the whale.

Adam didn't want Tom to hear him singing in a piping treble, even though it was badly cracked. So he lowered his chin and growled his way through the words.

'You're down in the bilges today!' Bungs commented, grinning.

After several more sea shanties, Mrs Worthington rose from the organ and beckoned to Pipaluk. Together they disappeared into the cabin she shared with her husband, leaving the others to smoke their pipes or chew their wads of tobacco and swap yarns and jokes.

'Have you had a woman yet?' Tom asked.

'Of course, I have!' Adam lied. 'Dozens.'

'Eskimo women give it to you for practically nothing, you know.'

Adam nodded knowingly.

Tom nudged him in the ribs. 'I'll bet you've done it with her.' He nodded towards the cabin into which Pipaluk had gone.

Adam teetered between truth and lie, stammering and turning red. He was saved by the cabin door opening and Pipaluk emerging. She was wearing one of Mrs Worthington's dresses. In her hair was a red ribbon. Adam stared at her open-mouthed. Could this possibly be the same person who had climbed the rigging with him, or knelt beside him mucking out the heads? She moved towards him and he suddenly felt shy and tongue-tied. Then she lifted her clay pipe to her lips and took a long puff and the old Pipaluk was somewhere there under the frills.

'Blow! Blow!' came the cry from above.

Whales had been sighted. Adam knew from his father that whales expelled a column of vapour from the blowholes on the tops of their heads. Men were grabbing their coats and bundles of warm clothing and rushing up on deck. Feet were stamping overhead, orders ringing out.

About a mile beyond the harbour entrance white plumes rose in the air like smoke from a distant city. The whaling boats were being lowered. Captain Worthington had decided the sea had calmed down enough to go after the whales.

Elisha gripped Adam's arm. 'I could swing it for you, lad . . . Get you in one of the boats – a chance to see what your father did best.'

Adam's mouth went dry with fear. He trembled all over. He wanted desperately to shake his head, but found he couldn't.

'Well?' The Ice Master's piercing eyes were on him.

He had to go. He had begun to understand just a little of why his father was drawn to the Arctic, and now here was a chance to . . . His head seemed to be nodding.

Chapter Eleven

'Lay on, lads! Lay on! Pull, I say!'

The headsman, Jesso Read, gripped the long steering oar in both his hands and coaxed his four oarsmen to greater effort. 'Pull, every mother's son of you! Crack your backbones!'

Jesso had once been a shipmate of Adam's father in the days before Nathaniel signed on with the *Triton*.

'I'll take the boy as long as he understands he's to sit tight and do nothing unless he's told,' Jesso had said to Elisha.

It was nearing midnight. The sun, a gigantic red ball, was resting on the rim of the ocean, setting the coastal ice ablaze. Crimson angels' wings spread across the sky. An iceberg in the distance glowed with internal fire, like the most magnificent ruby in all the world. In the open water a dark purple swell was running. The next wave swept towards them, high above their heads. The boat was borne upwards to ride a crest of burnished copper. Adam could see six whales, about half a mile away, sending up spouts of vapour. Each of the four ships in the whaling fleet had launched two or three boats which were pulling hard towards their quarry. In the harbour the ships were unfurling their sails and getting under way in order to follow them. Adam's gloved hands gripped the gunwale as the little boat plunged into the trough and they lost sight of their companions.

They battled through the rolling, ever-changing watery hills, rising, descending, rising again. The sun half dipped below the horizon, then began its ascent. Despite the bitterly cold air, the men had tumbled into the boat without wasting time over their warm clothing. Jesso allowed each rower to put on one article of dress in turn until all were completely clothed.

'Lay on, lads, we're closing. Plum duff for supper if you catch me that whale!'

The boat was narrow and pointed at both ends. Two large tubs held hundreds of feet of coiled rope which were attached to harpoons. Along the bottom of the boat lay the harpoons, lances, and all manner of iron implements whose purpose Adam could only guess at.

On the next rise the whale, a bowhead, suddenly seemed a lot nearer. It was moving slowly, straining krill through the long strips of baleen which hung from the roof of its mouth. It was about fifty feet long. Adam had once seen an elephant in a circus parade, but this... this was so much bigger, so immensely powerful and dangerous, so magnificent and beautiful, so terrifying and wonderful. He could hear the explosive 'Pooff! Pooff!' of its breathing. The air was ringing with a sound like a singing wine glass. They approached the monster side on.

'Softly now... Easy, lads, easy!... Spectioneer, stand by your iron!'

The spectioneer balanced himself on the small platform in the bows, harpoon in hand. When the boat was within a few feet of the whale, Jesso roared, 'Let him have it!'

The harpoon struck deep into the monster.

'Give him another iron!'

The spectioneer flung a second harpoon.

'Stern all! Stern all, for your lives!'

They backed away as the thrashing beast lifted its huge tail fluke and brought it crashing down, narrowly missing the boat.

Then it dived. To keep the line from running out too fast, Jesso took a turn of it round the loggerhead post. So great was the friction that rope and loggerhead began to smoke. Jesso handed Adam a bucket. 'Keep it wet!'

The bowhead took out 400 fathoms of line before it stopped.

'It's gone deep,' Jesso said. 'Lying on the bottom, I'll wager.'

The crew waited in silence. Every time they rose on the swell they could see the other boats engaged in the chase and the slaughter. The sound of an explosion reached their ears.

'That'll be the *Hope,*' said one of the oarsmen.

'Stow your whid, Jigger Lee!' Jesso thundered. 'There's only two people speak in this boat and you're not one of them!'

He turned to Adam and, in an altogether gentler tone, explained that the lead boat of the *Hope* had the new harpoon gun which fired a bomb that exploded inside the whale.

'The whale doesn't stand a chance. Costs a pretty penny, though.' He stopped and listened, feeling the line for signs of movement on the other end. 'Your father would have nothing to do with the unholy things,' Jesso continued. 'Said it would make the likes of himself no better than a butcher. An even contest, man against whale, that's how he liked it.'

Forty minutes later the whale surfaced with a whoosh. Jesso took a few more turns round the loggerhead. The line grew tight and the boat sped after the whale. They bounced across the waves in a shower of spray, yawing from side to side, shipping water over the gunwale. The crew bailed like mad to stop the boat being swamped. The harbour seemed to be getting more and more distant, and the *Rose,* which had been catching them up, fell away. The men hauled on the line, slowly drawing the boat close enough for the spectioneer to use his lance. He thrust it deep, churning it up and down until the whale spurted dark blood with every breath. Again they backed off. Mad with pain, the whale swam furiously round in smaller and smaller circles, beating the water with its tail.

The *Rose's* other two boats came over the crest of a wave and joined the fray. Two more lances went into the whale. It gave a tremendous shudder and turned over on its back. The men let out a great cheer. It was after three o'clock in the morning. As the clouds crept from crimson to pink, orange and yellow and then smoky mother of pearl, the sea all around the bowhead turned red.

Jesso playfully pulled Adam's woolly cap over his eyes.

'Well, Adam, what did you think of that? That could have been your father up in the bows, there. He was one of the best.' He laughed. 'Yes, it's all right to speak now. Anything's all right now we've caught ourselves a whale.'

Adam didn't know what to say. The exhilaration of the hunt, the raw courage of the men, sorrow for the death of a noble beast, the sheer cruelty and barbarity of it, they all churned around inside him in a confused jumble. That his father had fought with huge monsters at close quarters made him desperately proud and deeply disturbed.

Jesso made a hole in the whale's tail with a cutting spade and attached a towing line. The headsmen of the other two boats did the same while Jesso hurled friendly insults at them for their landlubberly slowness in arriving on the scene. The spectioneer cut the harpoons and the lance free. He wiped away the thick, sticky blood and began to sharpen them with his whetstone. Love and fear, thought Adam, love and anger, love and pain were like that, the one sharpens the other. The tired men bent to their oars again, pulling the gigantic corpse behind them. The *Rose* soon came up alongside them and the dead whale was secured by chains to its side. Three more whales, they learned, had been taken by other ships and another whale had been harpooned, but had got away. A boat had been capsized and, although the men were near to freezing, there had been no deaths.

Back in the bay, the work of flensing – stripping the whale of its blubber – had already begun as the *Prince Consort*'s boat ferried the *Rose*'s guests back to their own ship. Adam found himself thinking, not of the chase and the kill, nor of his father, but of Pipaluk. She was sitting beside him, wearing her usual clothes again. He wished he hadn't seen her dressed in Mrs Worthington's finery. It had forced him to think of her as a young woman and he didn't want to do that, it was scary and confusing. And he was angry with himself about Tom. The question had gone unanswered as to whether he and Pipaluk had done the goose and duck. Adam had a nasty feeling that, given a few more seconds, he would have lied and said he had. He should have found Tom and put him straight. But he hadn't. Had Pipaluk heard something about it, or guessed? Clearly she was troubled about something.

'They have no respect!' she burst out. 'Listen to them, they are shouting and laughing! Where is the hushed voice of respect for the dead?'

They looked back at the *Rose*. Slices had been made into the whale's skin and the underlying layer of blubber and a hook attached to one end of the cut. Now the carcass was being revolved by means of chains and pulleys so that the blubber, about two feet thick, peeled off in a long strip.

'And did they offer it fresh water to drink before its soul journeys to the underworld?' She gave a cry of anguish. 'The bones . . . they should be returned to the sea, where they want to be, not . . . not . . .' She buried her head in her hands. Adam could see that the whale's massive head had been winched onto the deck and the baleen was being stripped from a gaping mouth the size of Aunt Emily's sitting room. Seabirds circled and screamed in their hundreds around the boat, descending on the flayed carcass to tear at the flesh.

'Do the qallunaat know nothing? Animals only allow themselves to be killed because they are grateful that we honour them in death.'

The whale's tongue, weighing at least a ton, was being cut out of its mouth and dragged away.

'The whales will not come to the qallunaat if they do not respect them.'

'You speak the truth there, girl!' Elisha said.

On board the *Prince Consort* Quisby was fizzing with rage, the quartermaster was recovering from a fainting fit brought on by sheer terror and Qortoq was being held under arrest by the marines. Pipaluk was hurried to the guardroom to translate for him. She asked if Adam could go with her to help and that was agreed.

It seemed that Qortoq, single-handed, had eaten his way through an entire crate of 'Officers Only' canned quails in aspic. A hatchet was all he had needed to split the cans asunder. He did not understand how food could belong to anyone in particular. He thought of the ship as one big Inuit village where anyone, particularly a visitor, a guest, could wander into a tent or igloo and ask for food or simply take it if nobody was there. Besides, these little birds, they were everyone's property before they were caught, weren't they? Surely it was equally so afterwards? What belonged to the catcher was the joy of giving.

Qortoq had taken his crate down into the bilges. There he had spotted a tub half full of a warm kind of powdery snow. He had climbed into this and proceeded to demolish his trove of delicacies. As the quartermaster was inspecting his supplies in the eerie bilge, a white, ghostly figure had suddenly risen up in front of him. His yell and the clatter of his falling lantern had attracted three stokers who found a flour-covered Qortoq, hatchet in hand, bending over the quartermaster. There had been quite a struggle before Qortoq was finally disarmed and put under arrest.

'Theft is a flogging offence,' Quisby announced, tight-lipped.

'But he doesn't understand, sir!' Pipaluk objected. 'We Inuit share everything.'

'Even their wives,' said the quartermaster, who was making a good recovery, aided by a tot or two of 'medicinal' rum.

'Silence!' Quisby snapped. 'When I want your opinion, girl, I'll ask for it. If we don't make an example of him, the very first Eskimo village we come to, the ship will be swarming with light-fingered natives. One good thrashing and the word will soon get round.'

It was too cold to take Qortoq on deck and tie him to the rigging – too cold for the officers and crew, that is, who must assemble to witness a flogging. So Qortoq was taken to the lower deck, stripped to the waist and tied face down to a table. He submitted to all this with a slightly puzzled expression on his face. One of the bandsmen gave a long roll on the drums. A marine corporal stepped forward and laid on two dozen lashes with a knotted cat-o'-nine-tails. Although the lashes drew blood, Qortoq did not cry out. He lay with his eyes shut.

'My uncle is an angakok, a shaman,' Pipaluk said softly to Adam. 'He often lashes himself... even harder than that.'

'He does it to himself?'

In a whisper, Pipaluk explained that angakoks needed to go into trances in order to travel to the bottom of the ocean to consult with the gods. Dancing round and round, drumming, scourging their back, again and again – these were all ways to enter the trance state. This, according to Pipaluk's hot breathy words in Adam's ear, was what Qortoq thought was happening now. The qallunaat wanted him to predict the future and were giving him a helping hand.

When they released him, he slowly rose from the table and spread his arms wide before opening his eyes. He spoke in a deep, harsh voice, quite unlike his own. Pipaluk let out a gasp of dismay and clutched Adam's arm.

'What's he saying?'

Pipaluk shook her head. 'Oh, nothing much. I... I didn't hear all of it.'

'Tell me!'

She frowned and bit her lip. 'It was nothing, nothing at all.'

Whatever she wasn't telling him, Adam felt certain it was bad news.

Chapter Twelve

The smell of sweat, wet clothes, tobacco smoke and urine mingled with the odour of boiling salt horse. Adam was scouring pots in the galley. Ferret was doing his usual dance around Solomon. Peggy was an erupting volcano, his oaths pouring like molten lava over the absent quartermaster for his meagre allocation of rations.

'Am I feeding two mangy dogs or three score hungry men? Tell me that, boy?'

Adam kept his head down.

Qortoq watched Ferret, another of his puzzled looks on his creased face. His back had healed well in the two weeks since his flogging. Qortoq shrugged and went on with his carving. Already most of the beams on the lower deck bore strange Inuit symbols and depictions of animal spirits and endless carvings of combs. According to Pipaluk they were some sort of offering to Sedna, guardian of the sea mammals. When she was angry an angakok had to placate her by combing her hair. And she was angry because the qallunaat had not treated her whales with respect. It was rumoured that Quisby was strongly of the opinion that Qortoq had not treated the *Prince Consort* with respect and that, but for the intervention of the Ice Master, the old angakok would have been charged with defacing government property.

Adam wondered where Pipaluk was. She was off duty

just now. He knew her free times, just as she knew his. She would probably be playing one of her string games, making figures and stories from a piece of string – rather like Cats' Cradles which he used to play with Aunt Emily – only a lot more complicated. He wasn't sure quite how or when it had happened, but instead of avoiding Pipaluk he found himself seeking her out. He was glad of the storm that had blown them away from the Greenland coast, clear across to Baffin Island. It had given him time with her he would not otherwise have had. Now the *Prince Consort* was heading once more towards Greenland's northwest coast to reunite Pipaluk and her uncle with their own people. Adam didn't know how long it would take. He only knew that the old hands were saying there was more sea ice than any of them could remember for this time of year and that a blind tortoise with three peg legs could make better progress than the *Prince Consort.*

Skug passed the galley with an exaggerated swagger which meant Nightingale must be somewhere nearby. This was the moment Adam had been waiting for.

'Hey, Skug! What was the name of that whaler?'

'What whaler?'

'The one you was on that caught nothing, not like us . . . *Phoebe*, wasn't it?'

Skug swallowed the bait. 'No, fathead, it was the *Hebe*.'

Adam cast a glance at Peggy, but he hadn't heard the forbidden word.

'Are you sure? I could of sworn it was the *Phoebe.*'

'Listen, fathead,' Skug yelled, 'if I say it was the *Hebe*... aaagh!'

Before Skug knew it, he was flat on his back, Peggy's weight squashing the breath out of him, the dreaded Pegg's Purge being forced down his throat. A boy screaming for mercy and letting out the most awful gurgles and shuddering moans was more interesting than yarning or playing cards, so the men off duty crowded round the galley to see the fun.

Nightingale laughed cruelly. 'Go on, Peggy, empty the lot down him!'

'Nightingale!'

Adam could hear the pain in Skug's voice – far exceeding anything the Purge might be doing. Adam knew that feeling of being abandoned and betrayed. Why did his father prefer the Arctic to him? Why had he disappeared when Adam needed him so much? His mind could come up with all sorts of reasonable answers, but none of them soothed that raw, aching thing inside him. On an impulse he darted forward and snatched the black jar from Peggy's grasp and gulped down what was left in it.

Inside the chest which contained the dressing-up things, Adam wondered if he was going to suffocate. The trouble was, Bumble was sitting on top of it, pressing the lid tight shut, cutting off air and light. Shuddering from the taste of Pegg's Purge, Adam had fled to Great Cabin to escape from both Peggy and Skug. Best to let things cool down a little before he reappeared. He didn't have permission to be in Great Cabin, so when he heard someone coming, he'd climbed into the chest. Bumble, Quisby and Elisha were having a furious argument.

'It is my duty as Ice Master to warn you of the dangers of going any further north this year,' Elisha was saying. 'It would be wise to start looking for a safe haven to over-winter.'

Bumble's voice was heavy with sarcasm. 'Winter! Damn it, man, it is still August! Do you really expect me to disregard my orders to search for Franklin and tamely prepare for winter in the middle of the summer? What would the Admiralty say to that? Besides, I have the two Eskimos to return to their home.'

Elisha's voice was calm but icy. 'That was never anything more than an excuse to go north, and you know it. They could have been put on board a whaler long before now.'

Quisby spoke. 'I fail to see why we need to give up this early in the year, Captain McLellan. After all, we're the most technically advanced ship ever to enter these waters. Surely the ice doesn't hold quite the same terrors as it used to.'

Elisha started to say something, but Quisby interrupted him. 'However, I do question why we are going north. Franklin was heading west.'

'Which is precisely why we are going north,' the Admiral snapped. 'All the other searches have been in the west. And what have they found?... Nothing.'

'Not so,' Quisby declared. 'They've found relics and— '

'Trifles! The flimsiest of evidence surrounded by mere speculation! Clearly it makes sense to look elsewhere. After all, he could have . . .'

Adam had never heard Elisha so angry. 'You go north because there is more fame to be had in opening a route to the Pole than in finding what happened to those poor men. The public have lost interest in Franklin. They want new discoveries, new adventure.'

'Stuff and nonsense!' Bumble spluttered. 'It is within the terms of my orders to use my own discretion and judgement.'

'And your judgement tells you there is more chance of being a hero and of the knighthood you've always wanted if you go north.'

'This is intolerable! Quite intolerable! Why, if you were an officer and a gentleman . . .'

'But I'm not. Just a plain fisherman who knows the Arctic better than either of you. I may not have your refined ways, Admiral, but I do know that glory rings hollow when it is the motive for our actions.'

A feather began to tickle Adam's nose. He was concentrating so hard on not sneezing that he did not hear the rest.

Several days later, the band was playing on deck. The *Prince Consort* drifted through the mist on the stillest, most breathless day they had yet encountered. Adam marvelled at the almost perfect reflection of the slack sails. The engine thumped out a slow heartbeat. A hazy, palely shining silver disc hung over the main yardarm, multiplied by six satellite suns – reflections in airborne ice crystals. An iceberg, like a miniature alpine mountain range, loomed up. The *Prince Consort* turned hard to starboard and reduced speed to no more than a walking pace. Another iceberg appeared out of the mist, and another. Soon they were surrounded by a whole fleet of them, some higher than the mainmast. The strains of Handel's 'Water Music' echoed down crystal canyons and bounced from icy cliff to icy cliff.

A giant swan's wing, as transparent as glass, suddenly shattered into a thousand pieces. On a command from Elisha, the band fell silent; the engine stopped. The word ran round the ship in a whisper that the Ice Master judged these to be extremely old, brittle bergs, eroded below the waterline to the brink of imbalance so that even the vibrations of a ship could capsize them, while others might explode if you so much as whistled. Very, very quietly the boats were lowered, the oars muffled, the towlines attached.

Slowly and silently, the crew pulled the *Prince Consort* forward, winding through the ranks of the frozen fleet. Adam and Skug were counted as one rower and shared an oar. One proud smiling face, one scowling, disgusted face, side by side. They crept past a tall thin berg that rocked and hummed. Adam and Skug exchanged glances, united by the common danger.

Although Adam was pulling hard on the oar, instead of

getting warmer, he was getting colder. The temperature was definitely dropping. The water became viscous and tinged with pink. The loose brash ice turned to the consistency of cement. A blue fog of frost smoke rose from the ocean surface. When they were about a mile clear of the icebergs, a flag ran up the mainmast, recalling the towing boats.

Aboard the *Prince Consort*, a ferrety howl of anguish rent the still air.

'What's the matter?' Adam wanted to know, dashing up to Ferret who stood beside the rail on the upper deck.

'After all these years!' Ferret wailed.

He had taken his ring off for the rowing. On boarding the *Prince Consort* he had put it on again . . . except that he had unthinkingly put it on the normal ring finger – a finger he did not have – and it had dropped into the sea.

In the space of four hours the temperature plummeted by thirty degrees. The water imperceptibly solidified and blossomed with crystals. The mist froze on the deck, the mast, the halyards, the rigging, covering everything in white. Risking damaging the propeller, the Ice Master ordered full engine-power in an effort to bash a way through the newly formed ice and find open water again. But the *Prince Consort*'s progress became slower and slower until she stopped moving. They were beset by ice in the open sea, where the dangers of being crushed were at their greatest.

Chapter Thirteen

Boom! The pots and pans in the galley rattled on their hooks. Adam was used to the sound now and continued kneading the dough without looking up. It was the third barrel of gunpowder they had exploded since breakfast to shift a particularly large lump of ice. The plan was to cut a two-mile channel for the *Prince Consort* back to the shelter of the icebergs through which they had so cautiously made their way. Set solidly in the frozen sea, the bergs were stable. What had been a hazard a few days ago had become a possible means of salvation.

'Huh!' Ferret sniffed.

He sat down cross-legged on the galley floor and began to list all the things that had got them so jinxed up as to be stuck in the ice – Quisby eating the fish from the wrong end, Bungs saying out loud a word beginning with 'A' on the first of August, Piggy May cutting his fingernails on a Friday, and other serious offences of a similar nature, not to mention the lost ring. Out of sheer habit, Adam noticed, Ferret was counting them off on fingers he no longer had.

Both Peggy and Solomon were asleep. Peggy's hammock was slung above the black iron cooking range, clearing it by no more than eighteen inches. If you wanted to stir a pot you had to push the hammock to the side and hold it there – no mean feat when it was Peggy's considerable bulk you were dealing with. Solomon had buried himself in the ashes beneath the range, which, for the moment, meant one less source of bad luck for Ferret to worry about. Skug was in the galley, too. The hard labour on the ice had meant extra rations and a supply of hot drinks for the men. Skug had been drafted into the galley to help cope. He was unusually quiet. This was unfamiliar territory for him, and he wasn't taking any chances on crossing Peggy again. Even a sleeping Peggy was to be feared. Every now and then Skug would look uneasily at Adam out of the corner of his eye, still trying to figure out why Adam had been such a sap as to swallow the Purge for him.

From Ferret's recital of broken taboos and their resulting woes, Adam pieced together a disturbing picture. They were midway between Baffin Island and Greenland. There was no land for three hundred miles in any direction to offer a cove or a bay in which to shelter. In open stretches, strong winds and currents compressed the sea ice, until the enormous pressure pushed it up in ridges. Any vessel caught in this situation was in danger of being crushed. Some ships were lucky and, when pinched, were driven upwards to rest on the surface. But many more were crushed as if a giant hand were squeezing an empty eggshell.

Boom!

'What do they know?' Ferret grunted. 'Explosives won't help now. Only Lady Luck can save us.'

Out on the ice, the crew worked round the clock in the continuous daylight. Men were sawing at the ice with huge two-handed ice saws. Already the ice was more than a foot thick. The anchor chain had been laid out on the frozen sea and the anchor manoeuvred through a hole cut in the ice. When the steam-driven winch was operated, the *Prince Consort* clawed itself forward into the few, hard-won yards of newly cut channel before it froze over again.

Almost directly overhead something hit the deck with a tremendous thump. All three heads went up. There were shouts and running feet. Ferret knew what it was straight away.

'Poor blighter must of fallen from the topgallants at least,' he said. 'Dead for sure.'

Both Adam and Skug started forward to the companionway to see who it was.

'No you don't!' Ferret snapped. 'You'll stay here and get on with your work!'

There was a stir among the men on the lower deck who were not on watch.

'Bet it was Sawny Scott.'

'Nah, more like Nightingale. Only swapped his baccy ration for Bobby Dando's rum.'

'Floggin' offence, that.'

'Did it all the same, didn't he?'

Word reached them soon enough that it was indeed Nightingale who had been killed by the fall. A dozen men had been working in the upper rigging, chipping away the layer of ice and rime that was building up on the mast, spars and rigging. Nightingale had slipped, bounced once on the halyards and then hit the deck headfirst. Later in the day there would be a short funeral service before his body was committed to the deep.

'I'm sorry, Skug,' Adam said. 'I know he was a friend of yours.'

Skug twisted his features into a couldn't-care-less expression and shrugged. 'Not specially.'

The bread was baking in the oven, filling the galley with a delicious smell.

'Hot cocoa to the crow's-nest!' Ferret sang out.

Standing in the padded barrel at the top of the mainmast, a man was watching for any weaknesses or cracks in the ice which might be used to advantage. Each lookout stayed up two hours, with a hot drink carried up to him halfway through. Pipaluk usually went. She was agile and sure-footed in the rigging. She said it was because she was used to climbing the cliffs near her home to collect the auks' eggs. But Pipaluk was not on duty.

'You go, Skug,' Ferret said.

Skug went pale. He began to tremble. Asking Skug to climb the rigging, with a big drop below, was for him, Adam realised, the equivalent of going out on the ice when there were polar bears around. Some things were just too terrifying to even think about. And on top of Nightingale's fall . . .

'Well, get a move on!' Ferret yelled, thrusting the can of hot cocoa at Skug.

'Let me do it,' Adam said. 'I could do with a bit of fresh air.'

This time there was no uncomprehending frown from Skug, no suspicious stare, only a look of pure relief and gratitude. Adam was surprised to find that he felt relief, too – like one of his boils had burst and the pus was draining away, only this one was right inside him.

A thick fog shrouded the upper deck. Adam slung the padded, insulating bag which contained the can around his neck and began to climb the rigging. He went slowly and carefully, mindful of that awful thump when the body hit the deck. He'd been too proud to ask Pipaluk to go with him. Things always seemed twice as scary when you did them on your own. On the other hand, he had a big spot on his nose. He could see it without even having to squint. A flashing lighthouse would attract less attention. He knew he'd be so self-conscious about it he wouldn't enjoy her company. At least the ship was stuck fast and not in motion. Usually, the higher you got the bigger the arc the masts and their rigging swung through.

He rested briefly on the yardarm, then continued the second half of the climb up to the crow's-nest. Suddenly the fog was thinning. Adam emerged into a world of clear blue sky and dazzling sunshine. He felt like a caterpillar shedding its cocoon to become a butterfly. Through the blindingly white upper surface of the fog layer protruded the glinting peaks of the icebergs.

'About time too, lad!' the lookout hailed him. 'What kept you?'

It was Sawny Scott. His breath condensed in clouds, as if he was a dragon breathing out smoke.

'We thought for a bit you'd fallen,' Adam panted.

'Only for the temptations of the flesh, lad.'

'What's the point in being up here if the fog's hiding everything?'

'You know what Quisby's like.'

Adam handed over the bag.

'Thanks, lad . . . Climb in, there's just about room for a nipper in here. Saw a polar bear afore the fog rolled in. About half a mile off. Killed a seal lying out on the ice.'

Beyond the fog bank Adam could see the ice stretching away to the horizon in all directions, a vast frozen desert. How could anyone survive in this cold, empty, desolate place? It had been August, the same month as this, when his father had disappeared. There had been plenty of pack ice around his ship, but at least winter hadn't come as early as this. All the same, the whalers who knew him and who knew the Arctic had not offered much hope and Qortoq's answers to his questions had been evasive, as if he didn't want to hurt his feelings. Why he had ever thought he might find his father by berthing on the *Prince Consort*, he could not imagine. The whole thing had been a stupid idea. He felt like crying.

Sawny patted him on the back. 'There, there, lad. Don't take on so. I expect we'll come through this all right.' He handed his can of cocoa to Adam. 'Here, take some. It's not the first time I've been icebound, you know – one time it was for two winters running... and here I am to tell the tale.'

Adam gulped at the cocoa. His tears had frozen on his cheeks. 'Mr Scott...'

'Call me Sawny, lad. Everyone does.'

'Sawny, why do you keep coming back to the Arctic?'

'Apart from the extra pay for serving north of the circle, you mean?'

Adam handed back the can. 'Apart from that.' The cocoa was stone cold now and a thin layer of ice was beginning to form on it.

'When you're here, you curse it often enough. But when you're away from it, your heart cries for it like a lost child... the light, the scale of things, the timelessness...' He fell silent, amazed at his own eloquence. 'You have to have seen it in all its seasons and moods to know what I mean. Folk don't understand. Reckon that's why we old Arctic hands stick together.'

Adam nodded thoughtfully. Maybe he would never find his father, or know exactly what had happened to him, but perhaps he would find him in a different way. He would discover the sort of man he really was and why the Arctic drew him back again and again.

Two weeks later Adam was out on the ice with a sledging party. They had been to the nearest iceberg, two miles away, to chip ice to melt into fresh water. It was hard work pulling the massive, heavily constructed sledges, even without a load. When stacked with boxes of freshwater ice, it took a minimum of six people, five pulling and one pushing, to move them. Qortoq had shaken his head over them in disbelief and then fallen about laughing when he saw that, instead of dogs, men were being harnessed to them.

The temperature had dropped even further. In over two weeks of hard physical labour, the channel for the *Prince Consort* had been extended by barely three hundred yards. Then the freshly cut passage had begun to freeze over almost as soon as it was exposed to the bitingly cold air. As Ferret put it, they were 'well and truly glued up'. Captain Quisby had given orders to abandon the attempt to reach the icebergs and prepare the ship for overwintering. The furled sails had been taken down and stowed below decks. Spars had been carried up from below and an awning, which ran the length of the upper deck, rigged up to give shelter. Gangplanks had been lowered for ease of getting on and off the ice and sledges had been built.

Yesterday the sun had dipped below the horizon for the first time in two months.

And, for the first time since being issued with his clothing, Adam was glad that most of the items were too big for him. The straw in his oversize boots, he discovered, helped keep his feet warm. Already there had been one case of frostbitten toes, but Adam's toes had kept as warm as toast. And his jacket, which he had been embarrassed to wear because he felt so foolishly lost inside it, allowed room for extra clothing beneath it and for warm air to circulate about his body. He noticed that the caribou skin jackets worn by Pipaluk and Qortoq when they went outside were not tight like regulation naval jackets should be, but loose-fitting like his own.

Adam was at the rear of the sledge, pushing. Gardens of ice flowers and miniature forests of crystals crunched under the sledge's runners and under the team's feet. Misty vapours streamed from the mouths of the labouring men, their muffled breath hissing through the woollen masks that covered most of their faces. Steam rose from cracks in the ice where the comparative warmth of the sea below escaped into the cold air, catching the low morning sun and turning to a golden haze. The crystal fields gave way to an expanse of ice as clear as glass, through which Adam could see to the depths below where shadowy forms flitted about.

A noise like continuous gunfire made Adam's head jerk up. Cracks were zig-zagging through the ice. Adam could only guess at the enormous stresses causing it – perhaps a distant storm sending a swell running beneath the ice. Another bank of thick fog rolled towards them across the ice, its front edge like a billowing but solid yellowy-white wall. Soon Adam could hardly see the men in front. A fresh crack zipped through the ice with an ear-splitting sound. Adam slipped and sprawled flat on his face, banging his head. He stood up, dazed. Already the sledding team had been swallowed by the fog. They must have plodded on, heads down, unaware of what had happened. Adam's shouts were drowned out by the din of rending ice. He started to follow the tracks, but then they crossed a clear, glassy stretch which bore no marks upon it.

On the other side, where the ice was frosty and crystalline again, he searched left, then right. No tracks. He searched again, casting wider. Still no tracks. He tried shouting, but the fog seemed to deaden the sound and no answering shout came back. Adam had his eyes down, looking for the trail. Some instinct made him glance up. Immediately in front of him loomed a shape . . . a big white shape, taller than a man – a polar bear standing on its hind legs! Adam turned and fled. He was sure he could hear it behind him, although it was difficult to tell what was bear, what was cracking ice and what was his own panting breath. His loose-fitting boots seemed to flap on the end of his legs, slowing him down. He glanced fearfully over his shoulder as he ran, saw nothing, stumbled, recovered, looked again and, still seeing nothing, stopped.

He had no idea where he was. In his terror and panic he had given no thought to finding his way back to the ship in the fog. It could lie in any direction for all he knew. At least he knew he had to keep moving or he would freeze. He started walking, his eyes darting in all directions, expecting the bear to rush out of the concealing fog at any moment. He heard something . . . He stood rooted to the spot . . . pad, pad, pad! He wanted to run but he couldn't move. Out of the fog emerged Pipaluk.

'Pipaluk! Thank God!'

He couldn't think when he had ever been so glad to see anyone.

'I came out to look for you,' she said.

He threw his arms around her and hugged her close. They stood like that for several minutes, then she gently disengaged herself and gave him a big grin.

'Did you know that you have been going in a circle?'

Adam shook his head and gave a weak smile. 'I was lost... There was a bear...'

'No,' she laughed. 'No bear. We Inuit know when there is a bear.'

'How?'

She shrugged. 'We just know.' She squeezed his arm. 'This way.'

She couldn't resist teasing him a bit about being lost in circumstances in which an Inuit child of four could have found the way home.

'See the ice crystals, Adam, the way they grow towards the wind. Do you remember what way the wind blew all yesterday?'

He didn't. She shook her head in wonderment.

'And an hour ago there were geese flying south.'

He hadn't noticed.

'But the bear...' he began.

'A hump of ice. You must have passed it every time you have been to the icebergs and back again. How many times would that be?'

'Six,' Adam mumbled.

She stopped and drew a map on the ice, showing

where the *Prince Consort* was, where the hump of ice was and their own present position. Adam swallowed hard. He was used to being the one who knew things and who could be amused and condescending about her ignorance. It was hard to take when it was the other way round. But take it he could, because the memory of holding her close was a warm glow inside him.

Chapter Fourteen

It was early afternoon. Adam had found an excuse to be on deck for what would be their last sight of the sun for nearly three months. Only an hour ago the top quarter of an orange disc had appeared in the south-west above the ice pack, setting it alight as it slid along the horizon. The roar and growl of grinding, shattering ice was almost deafening. Colossal plates of pressure ice screamed and groaned against each other and heaved upwards in huge blocks, forming towers, labyrinths and gullies. And, in this chaos of ice, Adam saw something akin to the way he felt about himself – everything in upheaval, his body changing, hair sprouting all over the place, the strange feelings he had, the way his blood boiled and raced, the confusion of it all.

August had turned to September, then October. With the advance of winter, high winds and driving snow swept across the frozen wastes for days on end. And, as the days grew shorter, the ice tightened its grip on the *Prince Consort*. At first, it only held the vessel along the waterline. But, as the weeks went by, huge wedges of ice were pushed against the ship's side, until it was now nearly level with the railings. Down below, the main beams were bulging and bending under the pressure. Door frames were so badly distorted that the cabin doors would no longer close. Turpentine and resin were squeezed from the timbers to freeze in brown dribbles.

Adam jumped as, nearby, a sprung plank shot upwards, one end protruding from the deck.

Since last week, a new working party had been formed to carry supplies from the hold to the deck, and sleeping bags made of double blanket and canvas haversacks had been issued to all the crew. These were kept packed and ready to snatch up at a moment's notice should the order to abandon ship be given. The ship's boats, with runners attached to their undersides, waited on the ice in case they were needed. Peggy, Ferret, Skug and Adam spent every spare moment they had baking biscuits from the flour supply and adding these to the boats' provisions. Already there had been two false alarms. All essential items had been tossed over the side, only for the Arctic's crushing fist to relax again, so that everything had to be fetched back on board.

Qortoq had built himself an illuliaq, a temporary snow shelter, a little distance away from the ship where the ice was flat. Adam smiled ruefully to himself. It was the one thing he had thought he knew about the Inuit – that they lived in snow houses called igloos. But Pipaluk had told him that the Greenland Inuit only built snow houses when they were travelling in winter and that their igloos, their permanent homes, were made of stones and turf. Qortoq spent hours waiting, harpoon at the ready, beside the holes the seals kept open in the ice so that they could come up to breathe. About every two or three days he made a catch. Pipaluk had chosen to stay on board the *Prince Consort* and keep Adam company, although she visited her uncle frequently and shared with him the seal meat and blubber which she had missed so much.

The sun began to slip from view until only a thin glowing line was visible. Then that disappeared too. Qortoq was on deck, chanting in a monotonous nasal tone and drumming on a shamanic drum of stretched sealskin.

'Superstitious heathen!' Ferret shouted in Adam's ear. 'Don't know no better, I suppose.'

Adam didn't reply. He gazed in silence as the emerald-green twilight burned to purple and violet as the light faded. The emptiness seemed to go on forever. It was as if the crew of the *Prince Consort* were the only people on earth.

Three days passed and it was a Sunday again and time to get ready for Divine Service. Adam used to think of Sundays as a day of rest, a day when you might get a long lie-in. Fat chance of that on board the *Prince Consort*. Here it was a day for looking your best, a day of inspections and spit and polish. You could be punished for the smallest thing – like not having your hammock lashed up the correct way, or failing to polish the hinges of your seachest on the inside. That was Quisby for you.

'Above all else, it is order which will keep the men alive,' Pipaluk reported overhearing Quisby say. The most ordinary chores, he maintained, were an act of defiance against the chaos of the untamed wilderness. Secretly Adam agreed that almost anything was better than having time on your hands in the endless hours of darkness.

Small irritations easily grew into intense hatreds when people lived on top of each other day after day; suspicions and jealousies built up. But for Quisby's strict regime, the squabbles and fights would have been far worse than they were. Not that Adam voiced these thoughts. He joined in the griping about the discipline and the amount of work with the best of them. It was part of what kept them going.

The service was conducted standing. It was the only way the entire ship's company could be squeezed into the lower foredeck. From the stern, in Great Cabin, the Marine band played the hymn tune. In the dim light of the flickering lanterns, three score lusty males roared out the words, seeming, for all that, like mewling kittens compared to the awful voice of winter.

Thou whose almighty word
Chaos and darkness heard,
And took their flight;
Hear us, we humbly pray,
And, where the gospel's day
Sheds not its glorious ray,
Let there be light!

In the pause between one verse and another, they could hear the ice howling in rage, whistling and screeching. Adam was in the middle of the press of standing men. On one side of him was Pipaluk. Despite being acutely aware that his voice sounded like a cartwheel in need of oil one moment and a load of coal going into the basement the next, Adam was glad she was close. Since she had rescued him in the fog . . . since they had hugged, there had been a slight shyness between them. They had not touched again, but they both knew something had changed in the way they thought of each other. They often sat close, happy to be together, even if they didn't say much, while Pipaluk cut and sewed clothes for Adam from the furs Qortoq had brought with him to trade.

'You will need these later,' she said.

On his other side was Skug. For the time being, at any rate, there was a truce between them. In September, when the ice had still been flat, the crew had played football. Adam and Skug had got some good passing movements going between them. In one game, Skug had headed a goal from the ball Adam floated up for him. And in the pantomime which the crew had started rehearsing, Skug and Adam were the front and back ends of Daisy the cow.

'I'm the bit with the brains,' Skug liked to announce.

'And I'm the udder bit,' Adam would reply.

It seemed to Adam that Skug was less touchy and not so quick-tempered these days. It had something to do with the way Horse noticed the good things about people. He had come across Skug singing a popular song to a group of smirking sailors. The words had been changed to become a less than flattering description of the officers. Horse had given him a good dressing-down, but later, had complimented Skug on his excellent singing voice and suggested they sing a duet in the pantomime – Buttons, the Bad Baron's bootblack, and the front end of the cow.

A beam cracked and exploded like a cannon. The words of the hymn died away. Men stared uneasily at each other. Only Elisha's strong baritone kept the verse going until, raggedly, the others took it up again.

Move on the water's face
Bearing the lamp of grace,
And, in earth's darkest place,
Let there be light!

When the service ended, the men were free. Most of them went to the various evening classes which Horse had been put in charge of organising. Encouraged by Horse, Adam and Skug were both studying Mathematics and Navigation. Adam had expected Skug to sneer at the idea of taking classes. To his surprise, Skug was also learning to read and write – something he would never have done if he'd been playing the hard man in front of Nightingale. But Nightingale was 'feeding the fishes' and Skug could see that even tough old hands like Sawny were keen to better themselves.

Horse knew very well that many of the men would not join the classes if Pipaluk, an Eskimo and a girl, was there and likely to show them up. So he had asked Adam to continue his private arrangement with Pipaluk, she teaching him Kalaallisut, he helping her improve her English – not that Adam had needed much persuading.

'Are you going to Horse's magic lantern show when your class finishes?' Pipaluk asked Adam.

'I don't think so. I've seen it five times already.'

'I'll give you a different kind of show, if you like,' Pipaluk said. 'You can watch me talk the language of the hands.'

Adam knew she meant she wanted to show him some of her string figures. It sounded pretty boring.

'Good idea,' he said.

Sitting on their seachests, facing each other, Adam discovered just how fascinating a simple piece of string could become in skilled hands. Some of the more complicated figures required several strings of different colours and the use, not only of her hands, but of her feet and teeth as well. For Adam's benefit she did Three Dogs in Harness, which involved nearly fifty different manipulations of the string as the dogs pulled the sledge across the snow. Adam watched her absorbed expression, her dark, intense eyes, her nimble fingers and, for a few moments, he forgot the ever-present roar of the ice and the creaking, straining timbers.

Pipaluk did Two Ptarmigans, Moon Gone Dark, and Little Fishes.

'People often work the strings at parties to go along with stories and songs.'

'I don't think I could do anything like that in a million years!'

'It takes practice, Adam, especially one like Red Fox Running. That's really difficult.'

'Show me that one.'

She shook her head. 'I'm not ready for it yet.'

'Well, tell me the story that goes along with it.'

Pipaluk saw Qortoq approaching.

'I will let my uncle tell it and I will translate for you.'

'Once there was a fox, a red fox, a red fox running,' Qortoq began. 'It was not grey or white like other foxes. It was red and it was running. It was running from whatever you, who hear my words, fear most. Or maybe it was pursuing whatever it is you most desire in all the world. And the fox, the red fox, the red fox running, ran beside a female bear, Nanok, the Great White Bear of the North. The red fox asked, "How can I become white like you, so that I cannot be seen as I run across the snow?" "To change you must be born again," answered Nanok and she swallowed the fox. Some time later, Nanok gave birth to three white cubs. "Why do you have a big bushy tail?" asked the smallest cub. "Because," came the reply, "I am Terrianiaq, the fox."'

Adam lay in his hammock. He listened to the cracking and rumbling as immense forces pushed the ice up into new ridges. If anyone opened the hatch to the upper deck, heavy white clouds of condensing air rolled in. This, and steam from the galley and the breath of the closely packed men, caused a crust of frost, inches thick, to form on the timbers. A rivet gave way with a sound like a pistol shot. The tortured ship groaned, quivering and vibrating. Close to Adam's head, monstrous claws raked along the outside of the hull. Adam reached out and found Pipaluk's hand. Another beam buckled and broke. Somewhere out in the darkness an ice tower collapsed and crumbled to ruin. A huddled shape in a hammock spoke out of the gloom. 'This time it'll be no false alarm. Mark my words, this time the *Prince* is a gonner.'

'You said that afore, Jonah. Belt up and let a body get some kip.'

But the incessant noise, the sudden crashes and explosions, the constant fear and the pressing, suffocating, claustrophobic darkness made sleep impossible. Hour after hour, Adam, like many another, lay awake, listening to the slow destruction of the *Prince Consort*.

Chapter Fifteen

'Adam! Adam!'

Pipaluk was shaking him. 'Wake up! Wake up!'

Adam tumbled out of his hammock. In the dark, people all around were gathering their bundles and haversacks and making for the upper deck. The noise inside the *Prince Consort* was deafening. Every timber screamed in agony. The whole ship was juddering. Close by, a beam thicker than a man's body snapped with a report so loud that Pipaluk fell to the floor. Qortoq, who had dashed onto the ship to look for his niece, dragged her to her feet and pushed both her and Adam up the ladder. They leapt over the railing into the snow which was now no more than six feet below. Seconds later, the ribs of the ship cracked and gave way.

From a safe distance, Adam saw the two sides of the hull crunch together. The masts toppled like felled trees. The funnel collapsed and hung drunkenly to one side. The boiler exploded, sending jets of steam into the night air. In complete silence, the crew watched the destruction of what had been their home for the last eight months. Someone started to say the Lord's Prayer. Others joined in as the *Prince Consort* was overpowered by the ice. Thousands of rats streamed out of the stricken vessel and headed for the sledge-boats, only to be flattened or beaten back by pickets armed with shovels.

It was two o'clock in the morning. The stars were bright

in the sky. A half moon laid a silver path across the frozen sea. The icebergs, blue-robed monarchs, stood silent and aloof. Only now did Adam notice Peggy. He was wheezing with distress, his flabby body quivering like a jolted jelly. Ferret was fixing something like horses' blinkers round Peggy's eyes. Adam suddenly realised that Peggy had a fear of open spaces. In all the months they'd been aboard the *Prince Consort* Peggy had never once been up on deck. In fact, now that Adam thought about it, he had hardly ever left the confinement of the galley. Tucked inside his jacket was Solomon. Peggy kept his head lowered, his face buried in the cat's fur, trying to shut out the vastness around him. The surgeon had pronounced him unfit for hauling duties, much to the disgust of Quisby, who believed every person not working was a malingerer.

'Take your positions!' the boatswain ordered.

Now that the ship had been abandoned, Bumble had taken over command from Quisby. The men gathered on the ice had just learned where they were going. Bumble had decided to head for Coutts Inlet, nearly three hundred miles away on Baffin Island. If they succeeded in hauling the boats all that way, it would be a remarkable achievement, an epic journey.

Pipaluk turned to Adam. 'Wouldn't it be more sensible to camp in the shelter of the nearby icebergs and wait for the thaw to come?'

Adam said, 'Remember me telling you about the argument between Bumble and Elisha while I was hiding in the seachest in Great Cabin?'

'Yes.'

'Well, I think Bumble's decision to haul the boats all that way is because it will make him and the expedition look much more heroic.'

Each of the three boats was to be hauled by twelve seamen, petty officers and marines, with another six pushing at the sides and stern. Senior commissioned officers, as befitted their rank and dignity, sat in the boats as passengers. Junior commissioned officers and warrant officers had been told to walk alongside the boats but not do any hauling because, as Horse later told Adam, Bumble was of the opinion that 'for the men to see an officer and a gentleman behaving like a mule would be bad for discipline and morale'.

'What about me?' Pipaluk asked the boatswain.

'This is not women's work,' he replied and she had laughed at the silliness of it.

As for Qortoq, he was a law unto himself. Even Quisby and Bumble had given up trying to order him to do anything.

Adam was pushing at the side of the boat in which Bumble sat upright and straight-backed in the stern, his Admiral's cocked hat jammed on top of his woollen head-warmer. On either side of him sat an armed marine. Pipaluk and Peggy trudged along beside Adam. Ahead, the harnessed men strained and panted to shift what Pipaluk declared to be the most stupid sledge she had ever seen.

'Who's my beauty? Who's my beauty, then?' Peggy

repeated over and over, rubbing Solomon's head with his nose.

'All right, Peggy?' Adam asked in one of the rare moments when he had enough breath to speak.

'That's the thing, Adam. There's nothing more enclosed than below decks on an Arctic ship... and nothing more exposed than... Yes, that's the thing, one hell of a thing. I was going to hide in the wreck and not come out. Dying in there couldn't be worse than this.'

'Did Ferret make you change your mind?'

Peggy wheezed and fought for breath before replying. 'I didn't tell him what I had in mind. It was Solomon. I asked him if I should stay in my galley... you know, the saucers. He said "No".'

'Yeah, well, that was the right decision.'

'Who's my beauty? Who's my beauty, then? Who's my...'

'Shut that man up!' Bumble barked.

One of the marines in the boat leaned out and prodded Peggy with the muzzle of his rifle.

The ocean surface was a broken, jumbled mass of ice, full of steep ridges and gullies. Hauling the boats was an exhausting, almost impossible task. Hours were lost hacking out a road for the three sledge-boats, building snow ramps, or filling in crevasses. Adam strained to inch the cumbersome craft forward. He was dizzy with fatigue; his legs and back begged for a rest; his shoulders hurt. He wished with all his being that they would have to stop to clear the way ahead again. Then they did stop and he found himself whacking at ice boulders with a pickaxe. The pain seemed even worse and he longed to be pushing again. Ten more whacks and I'll take a little rest, just a very short one, he told himself. But he reached ten and the boatswain's eye was on him and everybody else was going hard at it. If only Skug would stop, or Pipaluk. She seemed tireless. She had seized a shovel without waiting to be told and now she was shifting more snow than most of the men.

'Rest!'

Men sank to the ground or bent over their shovels and pickaxes, chests heaving.

'Who's my beauty? Who's my beauty?' mumbled the blinkered Peggy.

Five exhausting hours later, they had succeeded in hauling the boats no more than half a mile. They made camp still within sight of the shattered remains of the *Prince Consort*. A working party was sent back to gather wood for a fire. Already the path they had laboured to make through the crazy ice was beginning to deform and bend and merge into the chaos. This would be their first and only fire. By tomorrow, if there was such a thing as tomorrow in the endless night, the way back to what had once been the *Prince Consort* would be wiped out.

The sailmaker had made six large tents from sail canvas. Spars had been converted into tent poles. In each tent there were nine men and an officer. Adam was in the same tent as Peggy and Ferret. The senior officers would sleep in the boats, over which an awning had been rigged. Pipaluk was not included in these arrangements because she preferred to sleep in the snow house which Qortoq would build for them when he returned from hunting. She wanted Adam to come too. He asked Lieutenant DeVilliers, his tent officer, for permission to do so, but was sharply refused.

'To go native,' DeVilliers told him, 'is just about the worst thing that could happen to a white man far from civilisation.'

Qortoq appeared over a ridge, pulling the light sledge he had built for himself. On it was a young walrus he had killed. It was unthinkable for a hunter not to share his catch with the community. First, with a speed that astonished Adam, Qortoq skinned the dead animal. Then, as the person who had made the kill, he took out the heart for himself. Since it was the quartermaster who had provided the iron with which Qortoq had refashioned the harpoon head, he received the next best cut; then came the carpenter who had found spare timber for Qortoq to make the sledge which had been used in the hunt.

'Remind you of anything?' Adam asked Ferret.

'What?'

'The way Daisy was cut up. You know...who got what bits.'

Qortoq stood back and, with clear gestures and a happy smile, invited anyone else who wished to do so to cut a bit for themselves. None of the officers came forward. After a pause, Ferret stepped up.

'I'll take some for Peggy – that is to say, for Solomon.'

He cut a chunk. Adam did likewise and thanked Qortoq in his own language.

Qortoq looked pityingly at the tents before starting to build his temporary snow shelter. When he had finished, he beckoned to Pipaluk and went up to Bumble who was sitting in the boat, studying a chart. With Pipaluk interpreting, Qortoq spoke to the Admiral. Adam was able to follow some of it, the rest Pipaluk told him later.

'Of course, a simple person like me knows nothing compared to the great leader I have the honour of addressing...'

'Yes, yes, get on with it, man! What is it you want to say?'

'This foolish person has the ridiculous notion that there might be a better way of getting to Coutts Inlet, or Kangerdlusuaq, as I, in my ignorance, call it.'

The Great Bear in the sky pointed with its left paw to an area where, most winters, there was flatter ice; and then, if they followed the bright star that is the nose of the Caribou Spirit, they would come to where the ice ridges ran in a north-south direction. Instead of crossing the ridges, up and down, up and down, as they had been doing, they could travel parallel to them for a large part of the way. In following this route they would have to travel three times the distance, but, in his experience, going in a straight line was seldom the quickest way.

Bumble frowned and snorted in irritation.

Qortoq looked him straight in the eye. 'Alas, you are a child in this country.'

Each day had seemed harder than the last. After a week of exhausting toil, they had progressed just seven miles. Nobody spoke about it. They all knew that, at this rate, their rations and their strength would run out before they reached Coutts Inlet. The heavy boats were both their only hope of salvation and their greatest curse. They needed them to cross the wide gaps in the ice and they would drown without them if there was a sudden thaw. But, with them, they might starve on the ice, miles from anywhere, because hauling them was taking so long. Adam knew this, but he shoved it to the back of his mind. Simply getting through the next hour, keeping going till the next break, making it through the shivering, hungry, so-called 'sleep' period, which seemed both endless and not long enough: these were what blotted out everything else.

Worst of all was the continual thirst. The ration was one pint of water per man per day. There wasn't enough fuel to melt more snow than that. Eating unmelted snow didn't work. All it did was make you colder, give you a stabbing pain between the eyes and make your teeth ache. To supplement his ration, Adam had taken to filling a canister with snow and strapping it next to his bare skin in the hope that the heat from his labouring body would melt it. The canister was in the sleeping bag with him now... empty. His mind dwelt on Aunt Emily's home-made lemonade, on the bottles of ginger pop you could buy for a penny at the little shop on the corner, on mugs and mugs and mugs of tea. Close by, Adam could hear Solomon purring and Peggy whispering urgently to him, weeping into his fur. Beyond his sleeping bag, beyond the tent, were hollow booms and echoes amplified by the silence of deep cold.

The boot thudded into Adam's back. 'Rise and shine! Rise and shine! . . . Get a move on, you layabout, show a leg!'

Adam groaned and dragged himself out of his bag to face another day.

The march seemed endless. Every hour they stopped for a ten minute break. Adam slumped against the boat. Raising his eyes he saw the Northern Lights. Magical curtains of colour flitted and rippled across the northern sky. As if whipped by a wind, fiery waves of light chased one another, interlacing and tumbling, constantly altering.

'They are the souls of dead children playing,' Pipaluk said.

'Have you seen Peggy?' Ferret asked with a worried frown.

'He was here a minute ago.'

A marine, the one who had flogged Qortoq, said, 'That ruddy moggy of his wandered off. He went after it.' He pointed away to the left where footprints, man and cat, sloped towards the crest of a pressure ridge and disappeared over the other side. Ferret, followed by Adam and Pipaluk, ran in their direction. Reaching the crest, they saw a long ice slab angling steeply down to a pond of open water, such as whales keep open by smashing the ice with their heads so that they can come up for air. Peggy was in the water, clutching Solomon in his arms. A strong current swept him under the ice. They could see his face staring up at them as he slid along under the surface. Then, either the ice thickened or he sank, for they could see him no more.

Chapter Sixteen

As they reached the crest of yet another pressure ridge, Adam looked over his shoulder. Below them twelve ghosts, wearing their best dress uniforms and ceremonial swords, sat stiffly at a long white table set with the Admiral's best china and crystal wine glasses. It had been Pipaluk's idea. After gaining only another twenty-five miles in three weeks, the officers had persuaded Bumble to lighten the load by jettisoning all those things that he had been convinced no civilised person could possibly do without under any circumstances. Helped by Adam and Skug, Pipaluk had made a snow tableau, dressed the figures in the discarded uniforms and laid the table like she used to in the *Prince Consort*'s wardroom.

Also lying abandoned on the ice, amongst the volumes of *Punch*, the brass polish and photographic equipment, were three of the six heavy tents. The men would be tightly packed in the remaining tents, but at least more bodies meant more warmth.

They laboured up a long incline. It seemed never-ending. Ahead of Adam, a man dropped dead in his harness. Thank God for a rest while they covered the body with snow and said a prayer. Adam stamped his feet to keep them warm. Was he the only person into whose head had slithered such a shaming thought? Even as he hated himself for it, he couldn't help wondering if he might get one of the man's blankets. The dead man's hood was pushed back. Adam saw that it was Sawny Scott.

Sawny's shipmates gathered round his burial mound, heads bowed. Quisby kept the service short. Three minutes was as long as anyone could stand still in the bitter wind – long enough for Adam to scan the bearded, gaunt, frostbitten, hollow-eyed faces and see the hunger and desperation in them. In the weeks that had passed since Peggy's death, exhaustion and hardship had given scurvy a chance to take hold. Some had blood seeping from the pores of their skin and large red sores on their faces, others had lost teeth where their gums had blackened and peeled away. How different, Adam thought, from the smart crew who had paraded on the deck of the *Prince Consort*, with the band playing as they proudly sailed down the Thames to the cheers of the crowd.

So far, Adam had escaped both scurvy and frostbite, thanks to Pipaluk's attentions. Neither she nor Qortoq, nor anyone in their community had ever had this thing the qallunaat called scurvy, she pointed out to him. Perhaps, if he ate the same food as they did, he wouldn't get it either. She had been insistent, almost forcing gobbets of raw walrus or seal meat down his throat. 'Like old sea boots soaked in kerosene!' he had pronounced, pulling a face. But her expression had been so fierce that he had swallowed. Now he regularly shared a meal with her and Qortoq and could get quite large amounts of blubber down without feeling sick.

Adam thought about Peggy being sucked under the ice, with only a swirling vortex to mark the spot. The march was like that . . . a downward spiral. The weaker they became, the fewer miles they hauled the boats each day, so that the rations had to be cut to make them last longer, which weakened the men even further. And the weaker they became, the more easily they succumbed to scurvy and frostbite. Already there were five men riding in the boats, unable to walk; among them Elisha, who had slipped and broken a leg. Another seven had to be taken out of the traces because they were too weak to haul. With Sawny's death, this reduced the number pulling and pushing each boat by four.

Adam looked at Ferret's gaunt, grim face. 'I'm worried about him, Pipaluk. On top of everything else, he's grieving for Peggy. I think he might be the next to die.'

'Maybe if you asked to see his tattoos, it would cheer him up.'

'I don't think even that would work.'

'Perhaps my uncle will know what to do. I'll ask him.'

'Take up positions!' came the boatswain's order.

Slowly, painfully, men climbed back into their harnesses. Horse walked over to the empty harness left by Sawny and put it on. This was in clear defiance of Bumble's order that no officers should haul the boats. A hush fell over the group. All eyes were on their Admiral, sitting erect in the stern of the lead boat. He stared straight ahead as if he hadn't seen. Nor did Quisby say anything. There was a pause, then another officer grabbed a harness and attached himself to a boat; then another and another. A cheer went up. The hauling teams surged forward into the starlit icescape with renewed energy.

A full moon sailed into the sky.

Breathing hard, Adam turned to Skug, who was pushing beside him. 'Do you suppose you can get moonburnt, like you can get sunburnt?'

'Make you go blue, probably.'

'Blue with cold, more like.'

Horse and Skug were now in the same tent as Ferret and Adam.

The lump in the sleeping bag next to Adam spoke in a low tone. 'When I die, will you strip me to the waist and leave me face down so my best tattoo shows?'

'You're not going to die, Ferret... not out here, on the ice.'

'Yes, I am.' He rolled over, turning his back to Adam.

Qortoq had come up with a plan to cure Ferret. Would it work? Adam wondered. He'd have to wait till tomorrow to find out.

'When I get back,' Horse was saying, 'the first thing I'm going to do is have a long, hot bath. Then I shall have a steak and a pint of foaming beer. After that I aim to push myself to the limits of physical inactivity.'

A laugh came out of the dark. 'Good on you, sir! Me, I'll just get groggified.'

'Silence!' DeVilliers thundered. 'Get some sleep, all of you!'

As arranged, Qortoq was waiting for Adam outside the tent, with a dead seal on his sledge.

Adam called out, 'Ferret, can you come out here and help us?'

'You think I'm mad? I'm staying in here, where I won't get my balls frozen off!'

'Qortoq says there'll be a little extra in it for you if you help him.'

Ferret popped out of the tent, closing it quickly behind him. 'What's he want me to do?'

'I'm not sure.'

They watched Qortoq slit the seal down the belly and pull out its stomach and intestines. Out slipped a complete fish which must have been swallowed whole. Qortoq indicated that he wanted Ferret to gut the fish while he got on with other things. Ferret took the knife which Qortoq held out to him. He opened up the fish and let out a cry of amazement. There, inside the fish, was his lost walrus ivory ring, his lucky ring.

'What luck! What incredible luck! What an omen!'

'It's almost unbelievable, Ferret!'

'Things can only get better from now on!'

Each time Ferret exclaimed over his good fortune, Adam and Pipaluk exchanged quiet smiles. Adam whispered his congratulations to her on her fine needlework. Not even a close inspection would have detected where she had sewn up a previous incision Qortoq had made in the seal. And, Adam thought, it was well worth bartering his penknife for one of Qortoq's several 'unique' rings which Pipaluk had then stuffed down the fish's throat before placing it inside the seal.

Early that day, they broke through to flatter, smoother ice. Suddenly the hauling became easier and they made a good fifteen miles. Morale rose. There was hope for them yet.

Chapter Seventeen

Qortoq told Adam, who told Horse, that a blizzard would hit them within the next twelve hours.

'How does he know?' Horse asked.

'He says he had a dream about it.'

'The Admiral isn't going to buy that.'

'But Qortoq seems so sure.'

'I'm telling you, Adam, neither Captain Quisby nor the Admiral are going to believe him. And, anyway, even experienced Arctic mariners say they're lucky if they can predict a blizzard more than an hour in advance.'

Which was exactly what Quisby did say when Horse reported Qortoq's warning. Adam was there to hear it because he was in the boat brewing up tea for them during one of the hourly breaks.

Elisha winced as he shifted his broken leg. 'Eskimos are seldom wrong about these things,' he advised.

Quisby stiffened. 'This is the nineteenth century, not the Dark Ages. Telling the weather is a matter of science, not something best left to primitive superstition.'

Elisha said, 'If I were captain aboard my own whaler, I would listen to him. I've seen the likes of Qortoq be right too often to take the risk.'

Quisby snatched the mug which Adam held out, hardly aware of him. 'Well, anyway, according to the chart, there's this island not far ahead of us. Should give us some shelter if this blizzard really does blow up.'

He turned to the leader of the expedition for his approval.

Bumble, who had been distracted and fidgety throughout the discussion, said, 'My father gave me a boat like this for my seventh birthday, you know. I pulled it on a string right across Big Lawn . . . a truly epic journey. And my toy soldiers were with me.' He pointed to a marine who was patrolling up and down outside the boat. 'Look, there's one now!' He gave a puzzled frown. 'I . . . I thought they'd all been broken or lost.'

Quisby said firmly, 'Lie down, sir. You'll feel better in a minute.'

Elisha took the mug Adam was stirring and gave it to Bumble. To Adam he said, 'Off you go! And don't say a word about this to anyone.'

'No, sir.'

'Good lad!'

One minute Adam was pushing the boat, feeling pleased about the good progress they were making, the next he was beaten to his knees, shielding his eyes and face from the sharp, stinging ice crystals sweeping across the desolate moonscape. Blinded, choking with the fine ice particles forced into his lungs, deafened by the roaring in his ears, Adam stumbled and crawled to the boat to help lift the tent out. Trying to control the billowing, flapping canvas and the whipping guy ropes was like trying to tame a kicking, bucking wild horse. One of the tents ballooned out and was wrenched from stiff, freezing hands to vanish into the night. Where was the island which could have sheltered them? There was nowhere to hide from the howling gale and driving snow.

At last the remaining two tents were up. Everyone piled in, shivering, numb-fingered, dazed by the ferocity of the blizzard.

'Like having your face sandpapered off,' Skug said, trying to control his shuddering body.

'And being flogged by ten people at once,' Adam added through gritted teeth. The pain in his toes as the feeling returned to them was excruciating.

'Did you notice Qortoq?' Horse asked as he breathed onto his stiff, claw-like hands. 'He and Pipaluk were building their shelter like it was no harder than making sandcastles on a sunny beach.'

Ferret was chewing on a corner of ship's biscuit he'd saved. 'More like a scrubbing brush than anything else,' he complained.

Adam smiled to himself. If Ferret was grumbling again, he must be in better spirits.

On the third day, with the blizzard still blowing and showing no sign of abating, a strong smell of rotting flesh began to pervade the tent. Someone's frostbite had turned to gangrene.

'Who is it?' DeVilliers demanded.

Nobody answered.

Assisted by Horse, DeVilliers inspected everyone's hands and feet, until the unfortunate man was found, one

Shoey McGuffin, with his three purply-green, swollen, stinking toes.

'I don't want to lose 'em, sir. Please don't cut 'em off!' he blubbed.

'You'll lose your whole leg, man, if we don't.'

The rum and the heavy pincers were brought out. McGuffin's foot was wrapped so that only the toes were exposed and poked through a slit in the tent until they froze again. Then rum was applied at both ends – down McGuffin's throat and to his toes. A crunch of steel on bone, a wild yell, a volley of curses, and laughter from those around.

'Any higher up and you'd have been Shoeless McGuffin!'

'Watch what you're eating in the dark, lads!'

Adam wondered if it had been like this for his father when his toes were amputated.

Pipaluk crawled into the tent. She found the huddled lump that was Adam and squirmed into the sleeping bag beside him.

'You shouldn't have come, not when it's this bad,' Adam chided her.

A seaman had been sent to get more supplies from the boat. Perhaps he had been picked up and blown away, perhaps he had become disorientated by the blinding snow and the wind that battered at the senses. He had not returned. A party of five, roped together, had gone out to look for him and had barely made it back to the tent themselves.

‘I’m glad you’re here, though. Very glad.’

‘I thought you might need warming up,’ she whispered.

They lay, fully clothed, in each other’s arms. She lifted her fur parka and guided his hands onto her warm, bare stomach.

‘Open your mouth,’ she breathed into his ear.

Adam obliged and she popped in something chewy, rich and fatty, but pleasantly nutty.

‘What is it?’

‘Muktuk.’

Adam had heard her speak of it before – the skin of kilaluga, the narwhal, a favourite delicacy amongst the Inuit. Qortoq had brought some with him and had been saving it.

Pipaluk said, ‘My uncle caught a big bull seal before the . . . the great wind . . .’

‘The blizzard.’

‘Yes. It was too heavy to drag onto his sledge, so he had come running to ask for help. When we returned to it, a bear had taken it.’

Adam lay next to her, savouring her closeness, their noses touching, their lips occasionally brushing as they chewed on the muktuk. Adam couldn’t remember when he had been so happy, or so excited . . . excited in a way he had not felt before.

‘Some people have all the luck!’ Skug growled from the depths of an adjacent bag.

Adam wondered if Skug was jealous. Were the taunts and the bullying about to start all over again?

Horse seemed aware of this too, for he started praising Skug for the rapid progress he had made with his reading and writing.

'Do you really think so, sir?' There was no disguising the thrill in his voice.

Horse started giving him a spelling test, always providing enough clues so that Skug would get it right. Flushed with the heady wine of success, Skug forgot about Pipaluk.

Adam lost count of the days as the blizzard blew with unceasing strength – days of boredom, gnawing hunger and constant thirst, and fear of being picked up and carried into oblivion by the sheer power of the wind – days that Adam wished would never end as he lay with Pipaluk. Without DeVilliers there would have been chaos and fighting in the packed tent. He organised a little walkway in the centre of the tent where, in shifts, the cramped inmates could stretch their limbs; he had a rota of four men at a time to hold onto the tent pole so that it would not be plucked from its socket when the whole tent heaved under the ferocious attacks of the howling monster outside. He organised a cooking area where the stove would not be upset by sudden movements and kicking legs, and he made sure the buckets were regularly emptied.

When they weren't dozing fitfully or following DeVilliers' routines, they talked. Ferret talked about working down the mines as a ten-year-old – the coal dust, the narrow tunnels, the darkness, the rockfalls. He had had no choice because his parents had signed a contract with the mine owner, promising his labour for the next seven years in exchange for a sum of money.

'Ran away to sea. Met Peggy on my very first ship and we stuck together since.' He was silent for a while. The tent shook. A loose guy rope cracked like a rifle shot, over and over.

Horse told them about his very first ride on a railway train when he was about six and the thrill of high speed travel.

'How the countryside flashed by! At times, we must have been going at very nearly thirty miles an hour! That's when I knew I wanted to be an engineer.'

'Don't seem natural going that fast,' Ferret said. 'Can't be good for you.'

'I think we'll go a lot faster yet,' Skug said. 'Engineering . . . that's what's going to change the world, isn't it, sir?'

'You're right there, lad, and you could be one of those engineers.'

Pipaluk said, 'We have learnt new ways too. I can just remember, when I was very young, we did not know how to build kayaks or make bows and arrows. We did not understand how useful they could be. Then a stranger from across the ice came to show us.'

There were some, she said, who did not want to change because it would be disrespectful to their ancestors not to do things the way they had always been done.

'But my uncle, Qortoq, who even then was a famous angakok, spoke about the musk ox. When attacked by hunters, they stood back to back in a tight circle and let themselves be killed by the spears.'

'Why didn't they run?' Adam wanted to know.

'You see, they had learned to defend themselves against wolves, but not against men and they have not been able to learn new ways, so they died.'

Almost as quickly as it had begun, the blizzard ended. Men crawled stiffly out of the two tents. Huge snow-drifts had built up on the windward side of the boats and the tents. There was a halo round the moon with two smaller false moons on its outer circumference. Horse was busy taking sightings of the stars and making calculations. He let out an exclamation and hurried off to report to his seniors. Although it was meant to be a confidential report, the word soon went round. In this part of the ocean, the sea ice was slowly drifting south. In the nine days they had been pinned down by the blizzard they had gone steadily backwards, losing all the northerly miles they had gained in over a week of hauling.

Chapter Eighteen

Despite Quisby's threats to flog any malingerers, moochers and skulkers, the number of sick men, unable to haul, had doubled during the blizzard. It was this that prompted Adam to make a suggestion to Horse.

'Sir, if we helped Qortoq with the hunting, there might be more food for us all.'

'I think he knows what he's doing without us interfering.'

'I didn't mean . . . I meant . . . Well, the other day he had to leave a seal he'd caught because it was too heavy.'

'I see what you mean, Adam. And someone with a gun, taken to the right place by an experienced hunter like him, might add to the pot.'

Horse took the idea to the senior officers, who agreed to the plan and picked Horse, Skug and Adam to go with Qortoq and Pipaluk.

Ferret insisted on giving Adam a lucky amulet to wear round his wrist.

'Could save your life.'

'Won't you need it?'

'Not now I've got my ring back. Like a miracle that was.'

Adam doubted if the amulet would do much good, but he put it on to please Ferret.

Skug said, 'You and me, Adam, we've been picked because we showed them at football that there's nobody faster on their feet than us.'

'More likely Quisby, DeVilliers and the others chose the two biggest nuisances they wanted out of the way.'

Skug said, 'I'm glad Horse is coming. Why him, though?'

'I think he's the only officer who doesn't mind being told what to do by an Eskimo.'

Elisha asked to see Adam before he went. The Ice Master sat in the boat, nursing his broken leg. It looked horribly swollen. Elisha wished him good luck on the hunting trip.

Then he said, 'I want you to know that your father is proud of you. If later in your life you discover there were things he didn't tell you, it was because he believed it was for your own good.'

Adam did not really understand what he meant. It sounded as though Elisha was a man who thought he was going to die, discharging some final duty.

Horse, Adam, Skug, Pipaluk and her uncle set off with the sledge and enough food for three days.

'All right for some!' shouted Ferret as the five hunters departed. 'Got yourself a cushy number an' no mistake!'

Skug called back, 'Now you'll find out who's been putting in the graft. Bet those tubs don't budge an inch without us!'

About half a mile from the boats they came to an iceberg, a crystal palace, jutting out of the frozen sea. They moved round it until they were out of sight and stopped. Horse unslung the doubled-barrelled shotgun from his back and took off his haversack.

'Since this is not a naval hunting party, but an Inuit hunting party,' he said, 'we are not bound by naval regulations in the matter of dress.' And with a flourish, he produced his caribou skin coat.

'Oh! That's funny... It's shorter than I remember it... How strange.'

Adam avoided Pipaluk's eye. She bent over the bundles on the sledge and pulled out the clothes she had been making for Adam ever since they became icebound on the *Prince Consort*. She handed him bearskin boots and trousers and a qulitsaq, a hooded long-sleeved jacket made from fox fur. Adam put them on.

'They feel so warm, so soft and easy to move in! They're wonderful, and beautifully made. Thank you, Pipaluk, I really like them.'

Pipaluk radiated happiness.

Only Skug was left in his coarse, heavy, woollen and felt garments. Horse took off the caribou coat.

'I'm giving it to you, Skug... as a gift.'

Skug went red and started to stammer something. Tears welled up.

Horse tossed it to him. 'Reckon you need it more than I do. The officers are in better fettle than the men they are supposed to lead – mostly because we've been better fed and haven't pulled our weight on the boats, and that's not something to be proud of.'

'Don't know what to say, sir,' Skug sniffed, shuffling into the coat.

Walking without a great big boat attached to him

seemed to Adam almost like flying. Under his feet the ice felt ribbed like sand when the tide is out. They moved through an infinite variety of blues and greys – dark gullies of midnight blue, deep Prussian blue where weird formations cast long moon shadows, streaks of glimmering silver, and tall, glassy sentinels of the palest turquoise and cerulean.

The indefatigable Qortoq, who was used to travelling at the speed of a dog team, set a fast pace which tested all of them, except the equally tireless Pipaluk.

'We're lucky he doesn't crack a whip over us,' Adam panted.

'Allut!' Qortoq grunted and altered direction. His keen eyes had spotted a seal's breathing hole. Squatting beside it, he peered into the allut which extended through four feet of ice, widening at the bottom to where new ice was forming above ink-black water. Qortoq sniffed deeply, then prodded the new ice with the end of his harpoon, to gauge its age and thickness. He got to his feet shaking his head. By his reckoning, the seal had abandoned this allut and would not return to it. This process was repeated a dozen times before Qortoq concluded that the seals had left the area. Perhaps the noise of the qallunaat tramping overhead had made them leave in disgust, perhaps they had fled from an orca, the greatly feared killer whale, or maybe the Lord of the Sea Animals was angry about something and ordered the seals not to let themselves be caught. They crossed a split in the ice, about three feet wide, which ran in either direction as far as they could see in the gloom.

Three hours later, and still having found no alluts in use, they stopped. Qortoq and Pipaluk set about building a snow house, declining any offers of help, saying they would be quicker on their own. Pipaluk unpacked the sealskins which Qortoq had kept from his previous catches. She laid these down on the snow platform which ran around the interior wall of the illuliaq and lit a little dish containing a wick dipped in seal oil. Not being properly cured, the sealskins gave off a strong smell.

After they had eaten, they rested on the snow platforms. It was surprisingly warm and snug inside their little hive.

When they woke, after five hours' sleep, Qortoq announced that they might as well return to the main group since they would find no seals on this hunting trip. But when they reached the break in the ice they had crossed thirteen hours earlier, they found it had opened up into a channel at least a hundred feet wide. Any thought of trying to swim across it was immediately dismissed. Even with their clothing on, survival time in that water would be about two minutes and their heavy garments would hamper them and drag them down. Horse climbed the highest hummock he could find and studied the channel through his telescope for as far as he could see in either direction.

'It just seems to go on and on,' he told them.

'Any narrow bits?' Skug asked.

'Not that I can see.'

They built another illuliaq and settled down to wait

either for the gap in the ice to close again, or for the exposed water to freeze to a thickness sufficient to bear their weight. There was no saying when either might happen, if at all. The immense stresses and strains on the sea ice were complex and impossible to understand or predict. And a stiff breeze was making the water choppy and unlikely to freeze.

Every hour Horse went outside and fired three shots in the air, followed by a minute's pause and then another three shots. This was the agreed distress signal. Perhaps their companions would hear it and send out a party to investigate. It would take days to drag a boat to the edge of the channel, but perhaps they could throw a line to the stranded hunters and let them haul food across. When there were two cartridges left from the box of one hundred, Horse said, 'Better keep the last two. Who knows what we might need them for.'

On the third day, Qortoq said that while they still had food and strength left, they must walk north. With every step they would go further and further away from their companions of the *Prince Consort* and from their food and fuel supply. They would walk, not towards land, but towards the middle of the ocean. This, said Qortoq, was their only hope. He scratched a map on the ice, showing them how they would intersect the route by which the Inuit regularly crossed from Greenland to Ellesmere Island by dog sledge. From both sides people made the journey to trade, to find wives, to gossip and yarn and enjoy the hospitality of another village.

'I cannot desert the officers and men with whom I've shared so much!' Horse protested. 'I must return to them if I can.'

'You have no choice,' Qortoq said.

'But you are asking these two boys to walk into the middle of nowhere, to walk to their deaths!'

'It is the people of the big boat who are walking to their deaths,' Qortoq replied.

When Horse continued to protest, Pipaluk burst out impatiently, 'Sir, the Inuit have no big cities to boast of, nor do we have libraries full of books or big ships with engines. But we survive where no qallunaat can survive. I did not see this before I came to your country where food is so plentiful that every day is like a feast. To have lived here for centuries is . . . is our great achievement. So when my uncle says you must do this thing, listen to him or you will perish.'

Looking at her flushed, impassioned face, Adam felt strongly drawn to her . . . and it scared him. To leave behind Elisha, Ferret, the boats, everything that was familiar was bad enough, but to enter the unknown world of love was really scary.

'We will keep walking,' Qortoq said. 'We will not stop. We will walk until we meet a dog team or until we die.'

His face lit up and he said something to Pipaluk.

'He says how can life be worth living if it offers no surprises, no adventures?'

Heads down, harried by a cold, stiff wind, they headed north into the Arctic night.

Chapter Nineteen

Keep putting one foot in front of the other, Adam told himself. Get a steady rhythm going, let the mind wander . . . anywhere, as long as it's away from this aching body. They had been walking for eleven hours and had stopped only three times, while Qortoq examined alluts. They had not been used. The seals had left the area.

Adam hated the sight of Skug's back. He'd been staring at it hour after hour, trying to keep up with it. Adam's drifting thoughts touched his father, the wonderful times, never long enough, when he was home, the hours spent waiting outside the pub for him so that he could ride on his broad shoulders on the way back. He thought about the bear which chased him through his dreams. He had talked to Pipaluk about it. She had told her uncle, who said all dreams have a meaning. Was that why he would sometimes look up and find Qortoq's intense, glittering eyes upon him? Images of his Uncle Jeremiah's place spun into his mind. He'd hated it, but how safe and warm and cosy that little attic room seemed now! Was he going to die out here in this frozen silence? He was too tired and numb to care very much. It would be like a long, long sleep. All he had to do was lie down and curl up and close his eyes.

Adam stumbled. His rhythm was broken. Every step became a struggle. His stomach cramped with hunger. A small bump lay in his path. The effort of lifting his leaden legs was too much. He skirted round it. The gap between himself and the others was widening. His legs were trembling with fatigue. He couldn't go on. Perhaps just twenty more steps... one... two...

Qortoq stopped. He said they were now in the middle of the broad corridor travellers used for the coast to coast crossing. They would simply wait until someone passed by, which could happen today, tomorrow, or next week and anything up to mile on either side of where they were. Nearby, in the lee of an iceberg, was a large snowdrift from which Qortoq cut blocks for building a snow house. He said they would have to take it in turns for someone to remain out in the open, otherwise they might not see or hear a team passing by in the distance.

They had been in the illuliaq for seventy hours and there had been no sign of a dog team.

'What's the time now, sir?' Adam asked from inside his sleeping bag.

'Half an hour later than when you last asked,' Horse said wearily. 'I wish you wouldn't keep asking.'

Skug said, 'Adam, are you sure you didn't miss anything when it was your turn to be out there? Maybe they went past without you noticing.'

'Of course they didn't! More likely it was you who missed something!'

'Cut it out, both of you!' Horse ordered. His voice sounded thin and weak.

None of them had eaten for a long time. After the seal

meat ran out, they had turned to the sledge runners. Adam had not realised, until that moment, that they were made of frozen walrus meat, coated with ice for smoothness. Next, they ate one of the sealskins used to cover the sleeping shelf. Being only half cured, it was still edible. Cut into small dice it was a tough chew, but better than nothing. Another seven inches off what was now Skug's caribou coat was sacrificed to the same end. Qortoq would not allow any more skins to be consumed, saying that the heat they gave as food was less than the loss of heat they saved as clothing and covers. Now there was nothing left, except a little of the seal blubber for the lamps which lit their shelter and over which they melted snow to drink.

'I don't think I've ever been so hungry,' Skug groaned.

'They come!' Pipaluk shouted from outside.

They wriggled out of the narrow entrance. Qortoq listened, his head slowly turning one way, then the other, to catch the sound. Adam thought he heard it, then it was gone. There it was again! Dogs barking and yelping.

Pipaluk pointed to her left, towards the west. Qortoq nodded his agreement.

Horse fired a shot in the air. The sound echoed off the iceberg. Then an answering shout came back. They could hear the sledge drivers urging on their teams and the sharp crack of whips.

'Ack, ack, arroo!'

Black smudges appeared in the half-light, then

changed into three dog teams, each pulling a sledge with two people on it.

'Where are you going?' asked the driver of the leading sledge, when he had brought his dogs to a halt.

'It is possible that one likes a long walk on the ice,' Qortoq replied, and that was all that was said on the matter.

'It so happens that we have a few poor scraps of meat, hardly worthy of your scorn,' said Inussuk, the oldest of the six Inuit.

'That means,' Pipaluk whispered gleefully to Adam, 'that they have plenty of meat and any excuse for a party will do.'

The six extra people squeezed into the illuliaq. When they took their outer garments off, Adam realised that two of them were women. The blubber stoves flickered and smoked and gave off their oily, fishy smell. Delicious odours wafted from the cooking pot. Outside, the tethered dogs whined and snarled. Adam was squashed between Pipaluk and a women with a heavily lined face and teeth worn down to the gums. Bundles of small sealskin bags hung above the simmering pots, warming in their steam.

'What are those?' Adam asked Pipaluk.

'Kiviaq. It is something only eaten when people get together.'

'What is it? What's it like?'

'You'll see.'

As was the custom, Qortoq and the other Inuit launched into details of their family trees for generations back. The illuliaq was beautifully warm with heat from eleven bodies and three blubber stoves.

'And Invuyak's father was Aguano whose second wife was Qinoruna, she who ran away with...'

Pipaluk was nudging Adam awake. 'The kiviaq is thawed and soft and ready to eat.' She handed him one of the sealskin bags. Adam opened it. A smell like overripe cheese greeted him. A bird's leg was sticking up. He pulled on it, copying the others. The carcass slipped free of the skin and feathers. Well-rotted flesh, coagulated blood and fat ran into his hand. Adam was so hungry he shoved it straight into his mouth. It was the strongest, most tainted meat he had ever tasted and somehow, exactly what his starved body craved. Later, Adam found out that kiviaq was made from guillemots. After they had been netted they were stuffed into sealskin bags from which only half the fat had been scraped, then stored under stones to slowly decompose and ferment.

'And the two sisters, Aloqisaq and Ivaloo, both married Maktak, whose father was...'

More kiviaq was passed round. Soon claws, beaks, bones and feathers were strewn all over the floor.

'And Akatuktuk's brother was Ooloo, he who was eaten by his own dogs when...'

The illuliaq spun and the voices merged into waves of sound which broke upon some distant shore.

Adam woke to find himself, well-wrapped in caribou skins, rushing through the starry night on the back of a sledge. The Northern Lights were flickering again, not in undulating curtains this time, but in darting flashes and long rods of light. Pipaluk was on the sledge ahead of him, chatting away to one of the wives. It must be more than three years, Adam realised, since she had last spoken to another Inuit woman.

'Ack, ack, arroo!' yelled the driver, sending his long whip flicking above the head of the lead dog.

As he lay there, his ear only inches from the hissing runners, Adam realised what was going to happen when the Inuit reached the community they were on their way to visit. With promises of payment at the other end, he and Skug and Horse would be able to take guides with sledges and dogs who would lead them south to where whalers would be overwintering in some sheltered bay further down the Greenland coast. And Qortoq and Pipaluk would go north to their own village. He would never see her again.

They stopped briefly to rest the dogs. She wasn't sure, but Pipaluk thought they would take about another eighteen hours to reach the coast of Greenland.

Then she shrugged. 'Imaaqa . . . maybe.'

Time could drag on forever when you didn't want it to and then, when every second was precious, like now, it seemed to vanish so quickly you felt sick with panic.

'Maybe we could travel on the same sledge,' Adam

suggested. 'Two of us together wouldn't be too heavy a load, would it?'

She smiled. 'Since you and I together weigh less than a young seal, I don't think they will mind.'

After about nine hours, the travellers stopped and built a snow house. They all piled in and began feasting and laughing and chattering as before.

With their bellies near to bursting and the walls shining with meltwater, Horse leaned across to Adam. 'You're very quiet. A penny for your thoughts.'

'Are they all going to die, sir? All our shipmates? Ferret and Elisha and everyone?'

Horse was silent for a while. 'It's possible. It's not just a matter of food. It's also a matter of morale and discipline and the will to live. They've got that on their side. But I'll tell you this . . . if they die, hidebound minds, arrogance and vanity will have caused the disaster every bit as much as the Arctic itself.'

Now that Adam knew what immense forces the Arctic could unleash, what extremes it was capable of, he feared the odds were against the band of men with whom he had shared so much. In his heart of hearts, he felt it more than likely that his father had died of starvation and exposure on an ice floe. In different ways, the Arctic had claimed the two people he cared for most . . . his father and Pipaluk. All too soon she would be returning to her own people.

The woman next to Adam produced several lengths

of string and began to make complicated figures.

'Can you do Red Fox Running?' Pipaluk asked. 'I'm still learning that one.'

The woman clicked her tongue. 'There is a new version now. I will show you.'

Between her spread hands and fast working fingers Adam saw a bear giving birth. But, instead of giving birth to a fox, as in the legend, out came a man with a big mop of hair and a bushy beard. The man stood up and ran across the frame.

'See Terrianiaq, the fox!' the woman crowed in triumph. 'See the fox running!'

'That's a man, not a fox,' Pipaluk said.

'But he is called Terrianiaq because . . .'

Was it possible? Hope, excitement, disbelief jostled in Adam's heart. Could it possibly be his father? With Pipaluk's help, Adam questioned the woman.

'Why did you show the fox as a man?'

'Because there was a man who arrived from nowhere who was like Terrianiaq, the fox.'

'You mean, because he had red hair and . . . ?'

'No. Because a bear gave birth to him.'

'But that's crazy! Tell her, Pipaluk, that's simply not possible!'

The woman shrugged. 'That is how it was. People saw it.'

'Who saw it? Who taught you this string figure?'

She pointed south. 'A long way.'

'Was this person, this new Terrianiaq, a qallunaat?'

'He was.'

'And did he have red hair and a red beard?'

'No.'

'No?'

'They say his hair used to be red, like the fox in the story. And, like the fox in the story, it turned white. When Nanok gave birth to him it was white.'

'Where is this man now?'

Again the woman shrugged. 'The ways of the fox are strange and the ways of the qallunaat even stranger.'

Adam gripped Pipaluk's arm. This was no made-up story. This was about a real man, a qallunaat who once had a red beard.

'It's my father, Pipaluk! It has to be!'

Chapter Twenty

Now Adam, Pipaluk and Qortoq were sledging north along the flat coastal ice. To their left loomed icebergs, set fast in the solid sea, translucent palaces with fairy-tale spires and turrets. To their right were high granite cliffs slashed by snow-filled gullies and frozen waterfalls. Qortoq's long whip hissed through the air and nipped the ear of a tawny dog in the middle of the team. The runners hissed and sang beneath them. A valley opened out, filled by an enormous glacier which descended to the sea. Where the glacier ended were huge cliffs of ice.

'Ack, ack, arroo!'

When the travellers had reached the community of seven families on the Greenland coast, Qortoq had done a deal. For a team of nine dogs, a sledge, piles of furs and skins and ample quantities of meat for himself, Pipaluk, Adam and the dogs, he exchanged the knowledge of how to find the wreck of the *Prince Consort*. To the inhabitants of the village the wreck meant immense wealth – timber in a treeless country, cordage, canvas, iron, coal, and the large quantities of supplies which had been left behind. Even if they only recovered a fraction of it, they would be rich beyond their wildest dreams.

Adam worried about Horse. He felt he had let Horse down. Horse, in the eyes of the Royal Navy, was responsible for him. Horse was duty-bound to stop him going north with Qortoq and Pipaluk. How could an officer explain to the Admiralty and the English public that he had allowed a sixteen-year-old cabin boy to go off on his own with a couple of Eskimos? So, while Horse and Skug were asleep, Adam had taken the shotgun and the one round of ammunition and slipped away. Qortoq and Pipaluk had been waiting for him outside the village, the dogs harnessed and ready to go. He wished he could have said goodbye. Without the shotgun to barter with, there was little chance Horse could persuade anyone to chase after him – not while there was all that feasting to be done with their visitors from Ellesmere Island. Once the feasting was over they would take Horse and Skug south because there were whaling ships and trading posts further down the coast and every prospect of being rewarded for their trouble. Besides, Horse's duty, above all others, was to return to England as soon as possible and inform the Admiralty about the fate of the *Prince Consort* and her crew so that a rescue could be organised.

'This is getting crazy,' Adam said out loud with a grim laugh. 'There'll be a search party looking for a search party looking for Franklin.'

As the nine dogs surged forward and the moonlit landscape glided by, Adam worried about finding his father. He had hoped, once Pipaluk was safely home again, to persuade Qortoq to take him south to the community that had invented the new version of Red Fox Running. If he could find the place, they were bound to be able to tell him more. Perhaps his father was actually there! It must be somewhere off that same bit of coast where his father had drifted away from the *Triton* on an ice floe. There were a lot of things he didn't understand. If the new version of the legend was really about his father, how could a bear have given birth to him?

They crossed a wide bay, aiming for a headland which jutted darkly against the skyline.

'Ack, ack, arroo!' Adam yelled, imitating Qortoq. But the dogs only put back their ears and howled, making Pipaluk laugh.

They journeyed for ten days towards Narlok. Adam had imagined that following the coastline would be a simple matter. He soon realised it was far more complicated than finding his way through the alleys and back streets of London. There were confusing clusters of islands to be threaded through, icebergs that looked like islands, islands that merged with the mainland and bits of the mainland that were easily mistaken for islands, channels with narrow entrances you could sledge past without seeing, and enticing gaps which looked like channels but weren't. Occasionally, to avoid going all the way round a large headland or peninsula, Qortoq would take a short cut across the land, the dogs wading up to their chests in the deeper snow. On the steeper slopes all three of them would push at the back of the sledge. Adam marvelled at Qortoq's ability to find his way through terrain he had only seen once before – and then it had been in a kayak and going in the opposite direction.

'We cannot get lost in our own land,' Qortoq told him. 'If we have done a journey once we can always do it again.'

Adam had already noticed both Qortoq's and Pipaluk's amazing memory for the lie of the land and the natural features around them. He saw, too, how Qortoq was alert to every sign. He would sniff the breeze, listen to the many voices of the ice, observe minute changes in the snow.

While they journeyed, Qortoq told Adam about the animals with whom they shared the land and the sea. Adam asked about the great white polar bears.

'Between Nanok and the Inuit there is a special bond,' he said.

'Well, they scare me more than any other animal and give me bad dreams, 'specially bad dreams, I can tell you that!'

Qortoq paused to crack his whip above the head of a dog that wasn't pulling its weight.

'Bears are curious, the same way we are. Like us, they always want to pick up things and look at them.'

'And they hunt the same animals we do,' Pipaluk added.

'Most important of all,' Qortoq said, 'we hunt each other and so we understand each other. Each has tasted the other's flesh and that is what makes a special bond.'

As they drew nearer to Narlok, Pipaluk's excitement mounted. How surprised they would be to see her! How nice it would be to see her aunt, Arnajark, again! And how little Navarana must have grown while she had been away! And there was so much to tell! Then Qortoq was swinging the sledge up a raised beach and into the middle of a cluster of eight or nine igloos. They had arrived at Narlok.

Their shouts received no reply. No dogs barked. No smiling horde tumbled out of the igloos to greet them. With a worried frown, Qortoq pushed his way into the nearest igloo, calling out the customary greeting as he entered.

He poked his head out. 'They are both dead! Old Akrat and his wife, both dead!'

Qortoq dashed to his own igloo which he shared with his widowed sister, Arnajark. Pipaluk and Adam followed. They found Arnajark and her granddaughter, Navarana, lying in a huddle together, their bodies emaciated, their eyes listless. In a faint voice, Arnajark told them that, soon after Qortoq had departed, almost everyone in the village had started getting a runny nose and vomiting. Then their skin had developed blotchy patches, followed by little red spots all over their faces.

'Measles,' Adam said.

'It is the same illness I had in England,' Pipaluk said. 'It is what my uncle Ululik died of.'

Adam remembered his father talking about whole villages of Eskimos being wiped out by white men's diseases which were new to them and against which their bodies had no defences. Even a common cold could kill them, his father had said.

'Did any strangers visit here before the sickness started?' he asked.

The old woman was too weak and dazed to be surprised at Adam's presence or notice his clumsy language.

She nodded, then closed her eyes and drifted into sleep.

Navarana lifted her head from Pipaluk's comforting embrace to say timidly, 'Visitors came from the south who had exchanged things with the qallunaat who hunt the big whale.'

'I think we should check the other igloos,' Adam said.

Six people had died, including the best hunter. Everyone else was ill and very weak. Many had developed chest infections and were wracked by bronchial coughs. Nobody had been well enough to go hunting for at least two months. As well as being sick, they were starving. Three weeks ago they had killed and eaten the last of their dogs. Since then they had existed on a few chunks of ancient, amber-brown blubber and hare's dung dipped in rancid oil. To make matters worse, as if sensing their defenceless state, a polar bear had twice raided the village. It had tried to break into an igloo and carry off the enfeebled person inside. Qortoq looked around until he found a sheltered place where the bear's footprints had not been erased by wind or snow.

'Large male. Lame in the left hind foot,' he announced.

While Pipaluk stayed behind to attend to the sick and make hot broth from the last of the food they had brought with them, Qortoq and Adam set out to hunt for fresh meat.

'What if the bear returns while we are away?' Adam said.

It was a chance they'd have to take, Qortoq said. Adam left the shotgun and the one cartridge with Pipaluk – just in case.

Qortoq drove the sledge dogs diagonally down the middle section of a glacier, steering by the light of the moon and the stars. Adam could see deep crevasses all around.

'Where are we going?' Adam wanted to know.

Qortoq pointed up the coast and out to sea. 'To find an aavequsaq.'

'What's an aavequsaq?'

Qortoq stopped and prodded a snow bridge over a crevasse with his harpoon.

'Why are you doing that?'

'You have much to learn. You must always test the strength of a snow bridge before crossing it . . . and an aavequsaq is where we will find walrus.'

He explained that it was a place where the ice was just strong enough to bear the weight of a man, but brittle enough for a walrus to break through it. Walrus did not have the seal's ability to keep a hole open, he told Adam. They preferred to smash the ice with their tusks, and surface.

They came to a particularly wide and deep crevasse. Sheer ice walls disappeared downwards into blackness. They moved slowly along its edge, unable to find a crossing place. After a great deal of casting about, probing and shaking of his head, Qortoq returned to a snow bridge he had already pronounced unsafe. He lengthened the traces so that the dogs and the sledge would not be on the bridge at the same time. With quick, light steps he scuttled across. The dogs went next, followed by the sledge. Then it was Adam's turn. Qortoq threw a sealskin line to him to fasten round his waist. Adam stepped forward, trying not to look down into the dark, bottomless chasm on either side of him. Suppose the bridge had been weakened by Qortoq, the dogs and the sledge? He took another step, and another. The next thing he knew he had collapsed on his side with one leg treading space. His right foot had broken through the snow. Qortoq was calling to him and hauling on the line. Adam heaved himself forward on his stomach. Cautiously he extricated his leg. Slithering forward, aided by the tugging line, he reached the other side.

Down on the sea ice at last, they made good speed to the aavequsaq. Qortoq tethered the dogs, took up his harpoon and spear and led Adam out onto the thin ice. Adam was carrying a thick pole of jointed ivory, with a metal spike on the end.

'I hope I'm not going to suddenly disappear!'

'Naw, naw!'

They waited in silence for what seemed to Adam like hours and hours. The dogs, some distance away, settled down, their noses tucked into their tails. They, too, knew when to be silent.

Adam couldn't help thinking about the bear, the one which had terrorised Narlok. It could return to the village any time and Pipaluk... One moment the expanse of ice was smooth, the next it was heaving upwards, shattering into little pieces, the head of a walrus rearing up. Qortoq was across the ice in a flash, hurling his harpoon into its neck. Adam drove his spiked pole into the ice. Qortoq quickly hitched the harpoon line over it before the walrus could dive. Both threw their weight against the pole as the line jerked tight.

When the animal stopped thrashing and floated exhausted on the surface, Qortoq killed it with a thrust of his spear. The water turned red with blood. Adam felt sorry for the beast, but at the same time he was flushed with success and proud that he had helped save Pipaluk's friends and relations from starvation. He started to say something in a loud, excited voice. Qortoq cut him short with an angry frown.

'Speak softly in the presence of the dead who have given their lives that we may live.'

Qortoq passed lines beneath the walrus' flippers and put the dogs to work hauling the dead bulk to firmer ice. Adam guessed there must be at least half a ton of meat and blubber, enough to feed the entire village until everyone was fully recovered. Qortoq handed Adam a knife. They removed their fur mittens and began cutting up the carcass. Whenever their hands became numb with cold they plunged them deep into the still warm flesh. Qortoq removed some of the half-digested clams and oysters from the walrus' stomach and crammed them into his mouth. His eyes rolled with ecstasy. He motioned to Adam to help himself. Adam knew it was stupid to be squeamish. He'd eaten tripe, hadn't he? And hadn't Aunt Emily curdled milk with rennet, the digestive juices of a cow?

Qortoq walked back to the scene of the kill and threw the remaining clams and oysters into the water.

'So that its spirit will not go hungry while it is returning to the Great Nature from which we all come.'

Adam tried to hand the knife back to Qortoq, but the old shaman wouldn't take it.

'It is yours,' he said. 'To be without a knife in this land could mean death.'

'Thank you, Qortoq. Thank you very much.'

The sledge was too heavily loaded with butchered meat and slabs of blubber to risk returning through the crevasses. They took the long way round, adding another four hours to their journey. About three miles from home they heard the shotgun go off.

'Nanok! The bear!' Qortoq shouted and whipped the dogs to greater effort.

Chapter Twenty-One

Blood spattered the snow between the igloos. Halfway out of an entrance lay a disembowelled body. The dogs, scenting the bear, were barking furiously.

'Pipaluk! Pipaluk!' Adam called, unable to control the fear in his voice.

'I am here.' She stepped out from behind an igloo, the shotgun in her hands. Adam could see she was trembling.

'Are you all right?'

She nodded. 'I think I might have hit it. I am not sure. It ran off.'

'Quick!' Qortoq shouted. 'We must follow it. Unload the sledge!'

They threw the meat to the ground and mounted the sledge.

'You too, Pipaluk!' Qortoq called out.

As they sped off, Pipaluk said quietly to Adam, 'We need three times as many dogs as this.' She explained that their job was to slow the bear down and to distract it while the hunters got close enough to hurl a spear into it.

Within twenty minutes they sighted the bear loping up a slope. Qortoq cut the dogs loose. They sped towards the bear and hurled themselves upon it, swarming all over it, biting, snarling, tearing at it. One dog was killed by a single swipe of a paw, another was tossed high into the air only to land in a ball, gather itself and rush back into the fray. Adam thought he could see a bullet wound in the bear's shoulder. A dog crawled away, its ribs exposed by a slashing claw. Pipaluk jabbed at the bear, making it rear up to its full eleven feet of height. Qortoq seized his chance. Running in, he drove his spear into its exposed chest. The bear roared, clutched the shaft and plucked out the buried blade. With lightning speed, ignoring the dogs hanging on to it, the bear lunged at Qortoq, catching him a mighty blow on the side, bowling him over and over. Qortoq sprawled in the snow. He did not move. The bear shook off the dogs. They lay panting, wounded and maimed, unable to continue the fight. The bear roared again, showing its huge fangs, and slowly loped down the slope towards the unprotected village.

'Stop it!' Pipaluk screamed. 'Do something to stop it!'

Adam knew he didn't have the skill or experience to kill the bear, and Pipaluk didn't have the strength. Grabbing the sledge, he launched down the slope, overtook the bear and continued on until he was about a hundred yards in front of it. Then he tumbled off the sledge directly in front of the beast. Flapping his arms and shouting, he started running towards the glacier which he and Qortoq had crossed earlier. The bear changed direction and charged after him.

A desperate plan had formed in Adam's mind. If it was going to work he had to be right about two things. He was depending on the fact that the bear was injured and could not cover the ground at its normal speed. It had been lame even before the battle began, and now it had been savaged by the dogs, wounded by a deep spear thrust and possibly shot by Pipaluk. And he was relying on the bear's natural curiosity.

Adam picked up the sledge tracks from earlier in the day and followed them, higher and higher towards the glacier. Each time he saw the bear gaining on him he dropped something – his handkerchief, the amulet Ferret had given him, then a fur mitten. The bear would arrive at the object and stop to sniff it and toss it about before resuming the chase. Without the mitten his left hand was becoming numbed and white. He kept it in the pocket of his bearskin trousers, but it hampered his running and upset his balance.

Adam glanced fearfully over his shoulder. The gap between them was dwindling. What could he throw down? What was left? His knife? No, Qortoq had drummed into him never to part with his knife. Without it you could not build a shelter or cut meat, even if you caught something. To remove his jacket or trousers would take longer than the time he'd gain when the bear stopped to examine them and it would mean certain death from the intense cold. Now the bear was even nearer. From his pocket he took the shellac case with his precious photograph in it. He let it drop. The case scuttered down the slope. The bear failed to catch it at the first attempt and turned to chase after it, pinning it with a claw on the second pounce.

On reaching the top of the glacier, Adam followed the sledge tracks through the maze of crevasses and over the tried and tested snow bridges. He had been slow in climbing the steep bit up the side of the glacier, and he was tiring fast. The bear was less than twenty yards behind and gaining on him. He could hear it panting and slobbering. At last, what he had been aiming for – the unsafe snow bridge. Taking a deep breath, he shuffled across it. The bear, so near to snatching its prey, followed. The bridge collapsed under its weight. In a shower of snow it disappeared into the abyss, its echoing roar fading to nothing.

But now Adam was stranded on the wrong side of the crevasse. It was a twelve-foot gap. On the flat, with a good run-up and wearing light clothes, he could have jumped it. But he was on the lower side of the crevasse with an uphill approach to the rim and he was wearing heavy furs. There was no question of taking them off. A cold wind had sprung up. He would perish in seconds without them. With difficulty Adam raised his fur jacket and stuffed his all but useless bare hand deep into his warm groin. He crouched like that, head down, hood up, trying to think what to do, trying to keep calm. The ice was too hard to cut into blocks, otherwise he might have built a shelter, or even some kind of ramp to put himself level or above the far side of the crevasse. His eyelids were freezing together. He rubbed his eyes with his mittened hand and blinked.

His father was running towards him, calling to him. He had a bushy beard like a fox's tail.

'Adam! Adam!'

That was odd. It sounded like Pipaluk's voice. What

was she doing here? Of course, she had to work the strings. How else could his father run towards him? And did he hear dogs chasing the fox . . . his father?

'Adam! Adam! Can you hear me, Adam? Look up, Adam!'

Adam looked up. Pipaluk was approaching on the sledge with the only four dogs still fit for pulling.

'Pipaluk!'

She could read all the signs well enough. She didn't need to be told the story. Jumping off the sledge she advanced to the edge of the crevasse.

Adam said, 'It is possible that one likes a long walk on a glacier,' and they both laughed.

'How is your uncle? Is he badly hurt?'

'His right arm is broken and several of his ribs, too, I think.'

'You got him back to the village, though?'

'It wasn't easy. The dogs were in no mood for pulling. But we got there in the end. He's resting now.'

Normally it was Qortoq who treated other people's illnesses and injuries. He had told her what to do and she had splinted his arm with flat straight pieces of whalebone.

Adam said, 'How can I get across the crevasse? The bridge was the only one that was any good and now it's gone.'

'I have an idea,' Pipaluk said.

The spears she and Adam had used were strapped to the sledge, as was the shotgun which she had still been clutching when they raced off after the bear. She untied them, opened the breach of the shotgun and rammed the shaft of one spear down the breach. The other spear she pushed into the muzzle. With the two spears joined by means of the gun barrel, she had fashioned a fourteen-foot pole to span the twelve-foot gap. She threw his mitten across to him.

'You will need this.'

Adam hung beneath the pole with his feet hooked over it. Feet first, he worked his way across. When he got to the middle, the pole sagged.

'Keep going!' Pipaluk implored. 'Don't look down!'

His feet touched the other side. Pipaluk grabbed his knees, then his waist. He'd made it across! Pipaluk threw herself on top of him, pummelling him and hugging him, congratulating him. As Pipaluk helped Adam to his feet, she slipped something into his hand. Adam couldn't see for the tears of relief that were filling his eyes and freezing, gluing them up again, but he knew the familiar shape of his shellac case.

When they got back to Narlok, Qortoq's first words to Adam were, 'We have another name for Nanok, the bear. We call him Tornarssuk, the one who gives power. Today Tornarssuk has given you a great gift. Go and look up at the Great Bear in the sky and give thanks.'

Adam went outside and did as he was bid. When he returned to the igloo, Qortoq said, 'Thanks to Tornarssuk you have faced your hidden fears, you have discovered the strength within yourself. Tornarssuk has shown that you are ready to hear the truth about your father.'

Chapter Twenty-Two

In some years, Qortoq said, the sea ice broke up much earlier than in others and the open waters extended further north than usual. In these years, the upernaadlit, the whalers, hunted in places which were usually closed to them. One such exceptional spring had occurred seventeen years ago. Qortoq paused and tried to fill his clay pipe from his tobacco bag. Seeing that he was having difficulty doing it one-handed, Pipaluk filled it for him. Old Arnajark helped herself to a fill, Pipaluk too. Adam, who had tried Pipaluk's pipe and been sick, shook his head when Qortoq offered some.

Qortoq spoke with his pipe in the corner of his mouth. 'It is possible there is someone here who claims to be an angakok, who knows nothing of cures or dreams, who has never travelled in spirit flight to the bottom of the ocean.'

Pipaluk's eyes flicked to Adam's face to see if he understood that this was another of Qortoq's over-modest remarks about himself.

'The people of Ilulissaat sent for me late one summer, seventeen years ago, to speak on their behalf to the Great Caribou Spirit who was angry with them for some reason.'

It was there that he had met Salamina. She had told Qortoq that she came from a community even further north than Ilulissaat, a place called Nuusuaq. At the end of the previous summer, the whaling ship of the qallunaat whom they called Terrianiaq had put into Ilulissaat Bay to overwinter. Terrianiaq had taken Salamina as his 'sea wife' to live with him aboard his ship during the long dark months while they waited to escape from the ice. The whalers often found companionship with Inuit women while they were away from their own homes, but Terrianiaq was different – he fell in love with Salamina.

Outside the igloo, the wounded dogs whined.

Old Arnajark said to Adam, 'They will either die or get better on their own.'

At least, he thought that was what she said. It was difficult to follow what the old woman said when she chewed bird skins and smoked a pipe and tried to talk all at the same time. Qortoq rubbed his sore ribs with his good arm. 'What I am about to say to you, Adam, I could not have told you until your encounter with Tornarssuk, the bear, but now you are ready to hear it.'

'What?' Adam's mouth was suddenly dry.

Shadows cast by the flickering oil lamps danced on the wall.

Smoke curled from Qortoq's lips. 'When the ice broke up in spring and the ship prepared to sail away, Salamina was expecting a baby.'

Adam drew a breath to ask the question which was burning in his mind, but Qortoq held up a hand to silence him.

'Terrianiaq had already departed before I met

Salamina. He promised to return the following spring. Many believed he would not keep his promise.'

Qortoq lay back, sucking on his pipe.

'The rest of the story I did not hear for many years because there were few alive to tell it.'

'Tell us, Uncle! Tell us!'

'Terrianiaq, the Red Fox, did return. By the time he reached Nuusuaq, it was late summer. The little boy whom Salamina had given birth to was eight months old. The whole community was in the grip of a white man's sickness. Terrianiaq arrived only just in time to be at Salamina's side before she died. He buried her and took the boy back to his own land. That boy was you, Adam.'

Adam flung on his outer furs and bolted from the igloo. He needed to be alone. The southern horizon glowed with a faint orange light. In a month the sun would return. He stood on a small bluff overlooking the frozen sea and the fleets of immobile icebergs, like ghostly galleons. Behind him were the dark, beehive shapes of the igloos. It was difficult to grasp what Qortoq had told him. His mind kept colliding with it, skidding away from it. All these years he had believed that his mother was an English woman who had died giving birth to him. He felt angry at being deceived. He boiled with rage. He wanted to shout and scream at Aunt Emily and at his father.

'I hate you! I hate you both!' he yelled into the night and burst into tears.

Somewhere in the mountains behind the village, a fox barked.

'Salamina,' Adam said out loud. His mother's name had never passed his lips before. He savoured it, repeating it over and over. He wondered what she had been like. Like Pipaluk, perhaps.

Then he was rolling on the ground, punching the snow, howling at the new moon, groaning aloud. The way he had taunted Skug about being a half-breed! He had never understood why it was something to be ashamed of, but his father and Aunt Emily must have felt that way. Why else had they kept it such a secret? The orange glow, which had briefly haunted the southern horizon, was fading. A dark finger of rock stood silhouetted against its final flush. In outline it looked like the gaunt figure and face of Elisha McLellan.

'I want you to know your father was proud of you,' Elisha was saying to him. 'If, later in your life, you discover there were things he didn't tell you, it was because he believed it was for your own good.'

Adam clung to those words like a drowning man to a raft. He sat up and realised he was still quite warm, dressed in his thick furs as he was. If he'd been wearing the clothing issued to him by the navy he would have been shivering with cold by now. Qortoq had demonstrated again and again that Bumble and his officers, despite all their modern equipment, their books and charts, were like helpless children compared to the Inuit in this bleak land. He had come to admire Qortoq and Pipaluk. What seemed a lifetime ago, when Qortoq was harpooning the walrus, and then when he was fighting the bear, he had wanted to be like that – resourceful, strong and brave . . . He veered away from the thought. There was too much to think about all at once. The kind of person he was, who his mother was, things about his father: all the neat little compartments he'd put his life into, all had to be rearranged.

He walked slowly back to the igloo, questions forming in his mind. Why had Elisha said those words to him? He was a close friend of his father's. He must have known about Sal . . . about his mother. And how could Qortoq be so certain that the white man he had met seventeen years ago was his father? There must be other whalers with red hair.

'Because,' said Qortoq, 'I met Terrianiaq, two winters ago, after Pipaluk and my brother, Ululik, departed with the qallunaat in their big boat.'

He told how he had been sledging south along the coastal ice. The clouds were hiding the stars and the moon and it was difficult to see. A pinprick of light suddenly appeared ahead of him which lasted for a few seconds before vanishing. He steered towards it and found a man with a bushy beard standing beside his dog team, lighting a pipe. The man was a qallunaat, but spoke Kalaallisut quite well. He said the Inuit called him Terrianiaq. He was heading north. They had talked.

'Was his beard red?' Adam broke in, although he thought he knew the answer from what the woman with the string had told him.

'It was white like his hair. And, if you remember the story of Red Fox Running, you will know that the fox became white.'

Terrianiaq had casually mentioned that he had been adrift on an ice floe, which was little more than a bare slab of ice. A polar bear had spotted him, alone and looking like easy prey. Luckily he had his big whaling harpoon with him and had killed the bear. The huge animal had provided more than enough food for the month that he drifted on the floe. And, equally important, it had provided shelter. He had removed its innards and crawled into the cavern of its ribcage. This had been his home for thirty-four days while the floe gradually dwindled in size as it melted. Then, one morning, he had heard shouts and, emerging headfirst from the bear, he had seen a party of Inuit in their kayaks.

After filling their pipes from each other's tobacco bags, Qortoq had told Terrianiaq he knew who he was and that he had met Salamina. He had asked Terrianiaq about his son. He was in the land of the qallunaat, Terrianiaq said, and his name was Adam.

Qortoq chuckled. 'For a qallunaat he handled his dogs quite well... Almost as well as a seven-year-old Inuit.'

'Why was he going north?' Adam asked. 'He was much more likely to find other qallunaat if he went south.'

Qortoq tapped his pipe and fidgeted with his arm. He was obviously in pain.

'Terrianiaq was a man wrestling with demons,' he said. 'And he had vowed not to return to his own people until he had defeated them.' Qortoq's eyes closed and his head nodded forward. His eyes opened. 'For a father and a son each to kill a bear, single-handed and alone, for both to meet Tornarssuk, that is something that will bind you together forever... What was that you said?... She was beautiful and loyal and they loved each other. I see her likeness in you when you smile.'

Chapter Twenty-Three

The nine people in the igloo lay in a semi-circle on the raised platform, feet to the wall, heads to the centre. It was early morning. Someone was moving about, hawking and spitting. Adam couldn't see who because a caribou skin was pulled over his head – probably one of the women because he could hear the chomping jaws and the wad of bird skin being shifted from one cheek to the other. Adam could tell that the person's boots were still half frozen and stiff by the way their owner hobbled and stomped. As well as Qortoq, Arnajark, Navarana and Pipaluk, there were four guests in the igloo. The more crowded the igloo the better they all seemed to like it.

Last night, one of the visitors had recounted how before they knew about kayaks, they had made rafts from inflated sealskins and paddled out to ice floes where there were seals. It was nagging away at the back of Adam's mind, although he couldn't say why.

Adam listened to the sound of frozen meat being chopped. He realised, with a jolt, that sometime in the past week or so it must have been Christmas Day. It had passed by and he had never noticed! Now someone was peeing into the big pail, adding to the supply of urine which would be used for hair washing, laundry and tanning. Living in an igloo, Adam thought, wasn't so very different from life on the crowded lower deck of the *Prince Consort*. Where were his former companions now? Probably still plodding painfully on, hauling the heavy boats, slowly dying of starvation, scurvy, exhaustion and gangrenous frostbitten limbs. Something slotted into place in Adam's mind. The sealskin raft. When they had been cut off from the *Prince Consort*'s crew by the wide rift in the ice, they could have crossed it. Qortoq had plenty of sealskins with him. They could have improvised air bags out of them and made a raft. Qortoq must have known it was possible. Had he known the expedition was doomed and that to rejoin it meant almost certain death?

Adam savoured the luxury of lying in bed, knowing that no marine was going to kick him and tell him it was time to get up. He thought about his plans. He had intended to go south and now he was hoping to go north to Nuusuaq. That seemed to be the way of it at the moment – so many things opposite to what he had thought they were.

Where else could his father have been going, but Nuusuaq? Of course, he might not still be there. It was two years since Qortoq had met him on the ice, travelling north. At least, Nuusuaq would be where he was most likely to pick up any clues about where his father might have gone. Getting there by dog sledge was no longer possible – there were not enough dogs and, anyway, Qortoq was not fit enough to drive a team. Adam knew he would have to wait until the thaw made it possible to travel by water in a kayak. The trouble was he didn't have a kayak and, even if he did, he didn't know the first thing about how to handle one. Qortoq had said something about Terrianiaq being troubled by demons. He didn't know what that meant and Qortoq would not say more.

Before they went to sleep last night, Qortoq had been repairing a harpoon, fixing the metal point, made in Birmingham, to the shaft fashioned from a narwhal's tusk. 'Everything has another meaning,' he said. 'Qallunaat and Inuit together make the best harpoon.'

Pipaluk was getting up now. He knew the sound of her quick, neat movements. Yesterday another baby had been born in Narlok, making three so far, to replace the six people who had died from measles. And four of the sledge dogs were expecting pups. With the reawakening sun, life was slowly returning to the stricken community. Adam thought about the crevasse he had bridged. Like the harpoon Qortoq had been repairing, the two spears and the gun barrel had been a combination of Inuit and qallunaat. Everything has another meaning, Qortoq had said.

'Tea, Adam!' Pipaluk called.

As the days moved through January, the glow in the southern sky spread further and further across the horizon, becoming brighter and lasting longer – deep violet, bruised purples, layers of lavender, crimson flushes and bars of yellow gold. And, as people began to get better, Adam quickly learned that the pulaar, the visit, was the Inuits' favourite occupation. The same neighbours came to visit Qortoq's igloo four or five times in the one day to gossip, tell stories, make string figures and consume large quantities of meat and tea. And, of course, Qortoq and Arnajark felt obliged to repay these visits as soon as possible.

These occasions, more than any others, exposed Adam's ignorance of Inuit ways, causing shocked looks, awkward silences or loud laughter. He was continually asking questions that were far too direct. He addressed old people in ways used only with the young, and greeted strangers with words meant only for people you knew well. Try as he might, he could not get the hang of the Inuits' self-deprecating way of saying things. On one occasion he deeply offended a mother by not licking her baby all over when it was handed to him. And, when it was time to go, his stumbling efforts to say the right thing invariably brought on a fit of coughing amongst his hosts. After a bit, he realised that everyone else simply got up and left without saying anything. What an embarrassment he must be to his hosts! Here, in Narlok, he must look every bit as ridiculous as Qortoq had at first seemed on the *Prince Consort*. There must have been plenty of times when Pipaluk could have criticised him or laughed at him. Instead, she quietly and tactfully tried to help him get it right next time. He felt ashamed that when she had been the one trying to fit into a different way of life, he had been so intolerant of her mistakes.

At one thing, though, Adam was a huge success – as a storyteller. He guessed rightly that his audience would want to hear about the animals they knew. It didn't need a great deal of imagination to 'Eskimoise' *Little Red Riding Hood.* A girl called Pipaluk was taking walrus meat to her grandmother's igloo when this wolf... Another great favourite he was asked to tell again and again, was *Goldilocks and the Three Bears*... Except that Goldilocks had straight black hair and the great big daddy Nanok growled, 'Who's been eating my seal?'

On one of these social occasions in Qortoq's igloo, while Adam was telling the tale of Jonah and the whale, a young hunter called Uvalu kept casting admiring glances at Pipaluk. As Uvalu was leaving, he placed an ivory comb on the ground near the exit. Adam had learned enough about Inuit customs to know that if Pipaluk threw the gift out of the igloo, she was rejecting Uvalu's advances. However, if she picked up the comb and used it, it meant she was accepting him as a boy-friend. Adam felt faintly amused at Uvalu's conceit in thinking he had any chance at all with Pipaluk. But Pipaluk didn't throw out the comb. She stared hard at Adam and left it lying where it was.

Adam waited impatiently for two things to happen – for spring to bring the break-up of the ice and for Pipaluk to chuck the stupid comb out of the igloo. Both seemed to be taking an awfully long time. The one he couldn't do anything about and the other... well, he was damned if he was going to even mention it to Pipaluk. If she was trying to make him jealous, he was going to have no part in her silly games. A massive show of not caring one way or another was just the medicine she needed.

As the return of the sun grew nearer, Adam turned both these problems over and over in his mind, getting no nearer to a solution. It was like having a lump of lead inside his chest. He longed for one of Pipaluk's smiles, but she had taken to avoiding him. He thought about the times they had spent together in Great Cabin, their heads touching over a book; about how she had found him when he was lost; how they had lain in each other's arms during the blizzard; and how she had followed him up the glacier, believing the bear was still alive.

In the igloo, Adam pulled out the naval jacket he had stuffed into a bag so long ago. He had changed out of it and into the furs Pipaluk had made for him when they'd started on the hunting trip. From it he cut the eight brass buttons embossed with a crown and anchor. He found a piece of thread made from sinew and strung the buttons into a necklace. He placed the necklace on the floor next to the comb and left the igloo.

As he stepped outside, he could see everyone gathering on the nearby headland. He joined the group of thirty or so people all in their finest clothes. He looked around for Pipaluk. He couldn't see her. The blues and greys of the winter darkness were suffused with yellow and green, then with carmine and gold. He spotted Pipaluk. She was wearing a fox fur cape, dog skin pants with stripes of coloured fur sewn onto them, and thigh-length boots of white sealskin. Adam had never seen anything so beautiful. Then he saw Uvalu standing next to her. Adam scowled and clenched his fists. He strode towards them. At that moment, everyone fell silent and faced south.

An orange-purple arc of sun lifted above the horizon, setting the icebergs afire before flooding the expanse of frozen sea with light and colour. Crags, rocks, icebergs, the standing villagers – all cast immense long shadows.

A great shout went up. '*Sainang sunain seqineq!* Greetings, sun!'

In keeping with the age-old tradition, they pushed back their hoods, baring their heads, and threw their gloves in the air.

'Seqiniliaq! The sun is appearing!'

Adam marched towards Pipaluk and Uvalu. He was opening his mouth to say something cold and cutting when he saw her necklace of brass buttons.

'Pipaluk!'

'Adam!'

Whether it was the rays of the newborn sun or her smile, Adam wasn't sure, but the world suddenly seemed brighter and rosier.

They found a quiet place and clung to each other and kissed.

After a bit, Pipaluk said gently, 'What's the matter, Adam? I can tell something is on your mind.'

'How am I ever going to find my father?' Adam blurted out. 'How can I get to Nuusuaq without a kayak? Not that it matters since I don't have the faintest idea how to use one.'

Pipaluk listened but said nothing. She did, however, just happen to wonder, the next day, how much taller than her he was. And, on another occasion, she found some reason for comparing the lengths of their legs. Adam suspected nothing. Then, one day, she took him for a walk which ended in a place where all the folk of the village were waiting for him.

According to Inuit custom, Qortoq explained, a major portion of the walrus meat and blubber on which the village had been depending while they were too weak to hunt, in fact belonged to Adam. He had taken part in the hunt and his knife had been the second to pierce the walrus' flesh. To him belonged the joy of sharing. By way of returning the favour, and in gratitude for saving them by killing the bear, the people of Narlok had quietly got together and made a plan. The outcome of all this was that Adam was presented with two newly constructed kayaks. One was for him and one for Pipaluk. He could not make the journey alone, they told him. It was not their custom for women to use kayaks – it was a hunting craft for men, but these were strange times. They could not spare a male companion for him. The walrus meat was almost finished. Every hunter would be needed during the summer to build up their stocks of meat again.

'You didn't tell me about any of this!' Adam said to Pipaluk, trying to sound stern and accusing.

'I had to wait until the Council of Hunters gave their permission... You do want me to come, don't you?'

'Of course I do!'

Her smile radiated joy.

'And I have persuaded Qortoq to teach us to kayak.'

'Terrific! Er... Is his arm fully mended then?'

'It's not strong enough for hunting yet... which is why he has time to teach us.'

Adam hugged Pipaluk. Now he would be able to travel north. What he'd find there, he didn't know.

Chapter Twenty-Four

Frost smoke issued from the rifts in the ice, red-tinged by the crimson ball hovering above the horizon. Adam and Pipaluk floated in their kayaks in a channel about ten feet wide – enough space, at least, to practise the basic strokes. Adam's wooden double-bladed paddle was tipped at either end with walrus ivory. He wore a waterproof sealskin top with sealed cuffs and a hood tightly drawn around his face. The bottom end of this jacket fitted snugly round the rim of the cockpit, making the craft watertight. With only the thickness of the kayak's stretched sealskins between him and the cold water, Adam was glad of the inner socks to his sealskin boots. Pipaluk had made them for him from rabbit skin with the fur turned inwards.

Crystal ice flowers bloomed in the water all around them. Illuminated by the low-lying sun, they looked like pink carnations. The very first thing Adam had learnt about a kayak was that you do not sit in it, you wear it. It was a tailor-made craft which fitted his hips, his knees, his feet and was controlled by his body movements every bit as much as by his paddle.

Behind them, children were playing their favourite springtime game of leaping across the narrower leads. A party of adults passed by on their way to the bird cliffs, carrying long-handled nets. The first to arrive in spring were the fulmars. Nobody really liked the taste of them, but anything was welcome after the winter monotony of seal and walrus meat. Next to return were the auks, whose bones were so soft they could be eaten along with their juicy raw flesh.

'Ready?' Qortoq shouted from the edge of the ice.

Adam raised his paddle, took a deep breath, wedged his knees against the main frame and deliberately capsized his kayak. The shock of the cold water on his face almost made him expel his breath. He waited upside down for Pipaluk's dark hull to glide above him. She had been on his right before he went over. He was still easily disorientated when he was upside down – everything that had been on your right was suddenly on your left. Ah! There it was! He reached up, grabbed the pointed bow and, with a rotation of his hips, flipped upright.

'Phew! Seemed like ages!'

Pipaluk was grinning at him. 'Well done! Not as good as Uvalu, though!'

Laughing, he splashed her with his paddle and she splashed back.

As the leads widened and the ice began to break up, Qortoq took them out into bigger and more open stretches of water. Qortoq was a hard taskmaster, making them practise strokes and rescue drills until they could do them automatically without thinking.

'You're worse than Quisby,' Adam complained.

'Your life may depend on it,' Qortoq replied.

He taught them the simplest kind of roll. From the upside-down position you had to reach up with your paddle, find the surface and perform a stroke that gave you sufficient leverage on the water to rotate your hips and bring the kayak the right way up. Even with his weakened arm, Qortoq made it look so easy and effortless, but Adam struggled with it for several days before his first successful attempt. Pipaluk learnt more quickly, probably, Adam thought, because she had watched people do it since she was a baby and also because being immersed in the near-freezing water didn't seem to bother her.

'No, I'm simply better at it than you!' she teased him.

Adam laughed. 'Well, neither of us will ever be as good as your uncle.'

Qortoq had been persuaded by Pipaluk to demonstrate some of the more advanced rolls – using a thin harpoon instead of a paddle, then with hands only, and finally without even one hand but just using his hips and body movement.

They had several attempts at fitting all they needed into the kayaks, loading and unloading them until they found the right space for everything. Any part of the kayak not occupied by Adam's body was crammed with provisions. They carried dried fish, strips of dried musk ox meat, and cubes of muktuk, the nourishing fatty skin of the narwhal. They knew they would have to supplement their stock of food by hunting, so they also had fishing lines, bird nets and a bow with a quiver of arrows. The bow, small but powerful, was made from laminated bone and sinew. There was not enough room to take a tent. Instead, tied to the stern deck and wrapped in waterproof sealskins, they had piles of caribou skins. To protect their eyes against the glare off water and ice, Qortoq gave them ivory goggles with thin slits in them. They reckoned they did not have the skill or the experience to hunt seal, so they decided to leave behind the harpoons and the inflated skin floats needed to prevent a dead seal sinking. A spare paddle each, some basic cooking utensils and the shotgun completed their load. Although there were no cartridges for the gun, Adam thought it might come in handy for trading.

In the days before their departure Qortoq drew maps in the snow and described the route as far as Ilulissaat. Adam wished he had pen and paper to copy the maps and make notes of what Qortoq was telling them. Pipaluk seemed able to memorise most of it. Adam, who was used to writing things down, found he could not remember the details with any accuracy. He could see that Qortoq was mystified as to how the qallunaat could have so many wonderful inventions and yet be so stupid and helpless.

Qortoq also gave them a collection of navigation rods. These were strips of bone or ivory on the edge of which had been carved the outline of each headland along the coast. On one edge of the rod was the succession of headlands as they appeared from a kayak travelling north, and on the other edge was how they looked travelling south. These navigation aids did not cover the area beyond Ilulissaat.

Adam knew that Nuusuaq meant 'big peninsula'.

He flourished the rods. 'There are dozens of big peninsulas along the way. If it's much the same beyond Ilulissaat, how will we know which big peninsula is Big Peninsula, if you see what I mean?'

Qortoq said, 'The village itself is small and easily missed.'

'So how do we…?'

Qortoq smiled. 'But I have heard that there are red cliffs behind it which can be seen from a distance.'

Pipaluk said, 'You have been beyond Ilulissaat, haven't you, Qortoq?'

'I was on a quest, seeking my first vision. No person can claim the title of angakok until they have experienced their first trance and their first vision.'

Qortoq told how he was with Aua, the greatest female angakok Narlok had ever known. She had taken him in an umiak, the kind of boat used by women, to some sea caves beyond Ilulissaat which went deep into the heart of a mountain.

'It was the blackest blackness I have ever known. Truly a place to meet the white darkness that accompanies a vision.'

Aua had told him that you could paddle through the caves and come out on the other side of the mountain into a different bay… If you were lucky.

'And what was the vision you had?' Adam asked.

Qortoq shook his head. 'The time to speak of it has not yet come.'

'What about saying where these caves are?'

Qortoq just smiled. 'I will not tell you where they are, but I will tell you that they are guarded by a dog with two heads.'

Then, one summer morning, they set out, skimming across flat water dotted with chunks of floating ice; gliding over the shimmering reflections of cliffs around which wheeled and called vast colonies of gulls, dovekies, fulmars and auks. Adam thought about his little attic room in London, of the Thames, dirty and confined, of the smoke-laden fogs. He took a deep breath and savoured the sparkling air. Here was where he wanted to be. This was his country.

Chapter Twenty-Five

Adam and Pipaluk kayaked close to the shore, their approach unleashing a blizzard of wings from cliffs and promontories. Seals, basking on rocks and small ice floes, slipped into the water as they neared. The two paddlers threaded between the outlying rocks, slipping between gaps too narrow or shallow for any craft but a kayak. They exulted in the way the sea pounded the base of the cliffs, sluicing between galleries of blackly shining granite, gurgling and sighing in caves and fissures.

Qortoq had advised them about the tidal currents. When the tide was going out the current flowed south along the coast for about six hours and when it was coming in, it flowed north for an equal period of time. The flow was at its strongest in the middle of the six-hour period. Their aim was to try and use the currents as much as possible, paddling when it was going their way and putting ashore to rest and eat when it was not.

They passed rock pools, limpet-encrusted slabs and shiny seaweed. Always on their left was the ice-flecked sea through which drifted the icebergs. They seemed to Adam like great glass sailing ships, like floating jewels, like crystal palaces . . . like nothing he had ever seen before. Qortoq had warned them not to get too close to an iceberg without being quite sure it was stable. They soon saw why. One of the biggest bergs started to rock and growl and tilt. It rolled over in a welter of bubbles, plumes of spray and hissing of trapped air. Up heaved the gigantic blue underside, a new island emerging from the sea, roaring into existence as water cascaded from it. A huge wave swept outwards, setting the neighbouring bergs dancing, making them groan and creak with internal stresses, and emit loud reports like pistol shots. Two bergs collided with a massive thump, grinding together with brittle, ringing booms.

At times, the icebergs and scattered floes provided shelter from the wind, so that the water was fairly calm. At other times, the two kayakers crossed exposed stretches. Then the waves would mount in size, rolling towards the shore to explode against the rocks. Separated from the moving ocean by only the thickness of a sealskin, Adam thrilled to the sensation of being part of it, of feeling its power and rhythm beneath him. Up, up they rose on the rolling green hills, down they plunged into the jade valleys. If he and Pipaluk were on different waves, they would disappear from each other's sight. Up, up again. Adam spotted the flashing top of Pipaluk's blade before it sank from view. Further out to sea, three beluga whales, their gleaming, ivory-white bodies just breaking the surface, were also making their way north.

Ahead, a glacier jutted magnificent ice cliffs into the ocean. Adam wanted to paddle close beneath them to glory in their spectacular beauty, but Pipaluk was adamant they should swing out to sea and give the glacier a wide berth.

'Where do you think all the icebergs around here have

come from?' she demanded. 'They have broken off the end of that glacier!'

'I suppose you're right,' Adam conceded.

They were about a quarter of a mile offshore when a whole section of the glacier's advancing edge, millions of tons of ice, split off with a roar and tumbled into the sea. A huge wash, like a tidal wave, swept outwards. A great wall of water rushed towards them, curling and hissing at the top. Adam faced into it, praying that this would not be the moment it chose to break. His bows rose, pointing higher and higher until he felt he was going to loop over backwards. He leant forward trying to punch through the crest. Spray enveloped him, blinding him, then he was sliding down the wave's gentler, reverse slope, whooping with excitement, looking around for Pipaluk. There she was, to his right.

'Just as well I insisted we didn't get too close,' Adam shouted and was rewarded with a fierce glare which turned into one of her wide smiles.

With the tide beginning to run against them, they stopped in a small bay, backed by barren snow-patched slopes. The sky was still blue-green, although it must have been nearly midnight. The beach was crowded with stranded icebergs – little ones, as transparent as glass, lying about at all angles. Beyond a line of dried seaweed of startling pink, a caribou's tracks ran the length of the sickle of sand. Adam and Pipaluk carried the kayaks up the beach and onto a barren plateau beyond. They had not forgotten the tidal wave. Another one could sweep them away if they camped too close to the water. They collected small boulders – no easy task in a landscape scraped to the bare bones – and built two low walls onto which the kayaks were lifted. Across these they draped the sealskins so that their sides hung down, forming a little shelter. Inside this they spread out their caribou skin bedding. With their damp outer garments hanging up to dry, the two voyagers lay side by side, snug in their shelter.

In the breathless, mist-shrouded morning they launched the kayaks. They paddled into the mist, pushing through shoals of waxing suns, gliding across a liquid mirror, marvelling at the almost perfect reflections. Adam saw his own face in the water, the first time he had seen it since . . . since when? Since being on the *Prince Consort*. It was a young man's face, not a boy's. All that agonising about his spots, his changing body, his silly voice . . . he'd been so completely absorbed by the struggle for survival, by hunger and danger and a thousand new experiences and new things to learn that he had grown up and never noticed it. Now that he came to think of it, his voice was deeper all the time, not just sometimes. And the thin, wispy hairs on his lip and chin were similar to Qortoq's. They were not a failed beard, but normal for Inuit men. Some time ago he must have passed his seventeenth birthday without being aware of it. He laughed out loud and gave his reflection a friendly smack with his paddle.

The mist thickened, so that sea and sky merged until they felt they were floating in a dimension of their own. Giant sapphires loomed through the mist, radiating an astonishing blue, outliers of the icebergs that choked the mouth of the channel they were heading for.

'Like carriages in The Mall, all held up by an accident,' Adam remarked and was pleased that Pipaluk knew what he meant.

They wound their way through an archipelago of turquoise, cobalt, pearl and emerald islands. The air chilled noticeably. The muffled roar of capsizing bergs filtered through the mist. Occasionally a swell rolled through the assembled ranks, rumour of the unseen event. Anything that looked at all unstable they hurried past or tried to give as wide a berth as possible – a difficult thing to do in this crowded water.

Day after day they paddled. There were spells when it was as calm and still as it had been in the channel, and there were other days when it was too rough to put to sea. They passed the last headland on the first navigation rod and started on the second rod. Sometimes hail beat a tattoo upon their decks and cratered the water all around; sometimes they pushed into a stiff breeze, at other times the wind wafted them along. Occasionally they took a break from paddling to fish or net birds and collect eggs. Adam's hands became hardened to the paddle, his face as brown as any Inuit's, his shoulders broader.

Once, a whale surfaced beside them; and twice, with a polar bear swimming towards them, they had paddled faster than they'd thought possible. Gradually the miles went by and the unknown things which waited in the north drew nearer.

Chapter Twenty-Six

An orange stain spread across the dawn sky. The tallest iceberg blushed at the touch of the sun's first ray. A beacon of light picked out another peak in lilac and green. A third sprang into golden life. Adam and Pipaluk were making an early start in order to catch the flood tide. Adam stamped his feet and chewed on the last of the seal blubber. He couldn't imagine how he had once thought porridge a sustaining breakfast for a cold morning. Now it seemed like thin pap with no real fuel in it at all. Yesterday they had reached Ilulissaat and found it deserted, the turf and stone igloos fallen into disrepair. How long ago the village had been abandoned, Adam couldn't say. Perhaps the same epidemic which killed his mother was the cause, or perhaps famine or some other disaster had struck the community. Adam wandered through the ruins, past heaps of bleached seal and walrus bones, trying to imagine his mother and father together in this place. How had it seemed, he wondered, through their eyes?

Ilulissaat was the last feature on their second navigation rod and on the map Qortoq had drawn in the snow. They had been hoping to get more information there. Now they would have to find their way without any help. In this complex coastline there were scores of peninsulas and, for all they knew, the village of Nuusuaq could be on any one of them. Day after day they searched and found no sign of red cliffs or any habitation.

'We'll never find Nuusuaq, or my father!' Adam groaned in despair.

'Keep looking,' Pipaluk said. 'You never know what's round the next corner.'

The sky was grey, the sea leaden and lumpy. The wind, straight off the interior icecap, was bitterly cold. They were crossing a wide and open stretch of water from the headland of one peninsula to the next. Adam had felt sure the peninsula behind them was going to be the one they were looking for. But there had been no red cliffs, no cluster of little igloos, one of which could be his father's. Without warning the wind doubled in strength, then doubled again, whipping the sea into a heaving frenzy, hurling spindrift horizontally through the air.

Tons of solid grey sea, curling at the edges, swept towards Adam. Up rose his bows, up to where the shrieking wind would have torn the paddle from his grasp had he not clung to it with all his strength, up to where the spume was driven blindingly into his face. Then the downward plunge into a deep grey gulf and the next wave looming over him, way above his head.

Another advancing wall of water, and another; never-ending ranks of waves, each one as menacing as the one before. He tried looking around for Pipaluk, but the waves demanded all his attention. He risked a glance to his right. She wasn't there. A breaking crest slapped him in the face, making him gasp. On the next crest he took a quick look over his left shoulder. No sign of her. An extra large chunk of water struck him in the chest, sending him skidding sideways, toppling over. Without even thinking what to do, he rolled up again. Thank you, Qortoq, for teaching me, thank you for making me practise till I cursed you. Where was she? Not even an upturned hull in sight.

Adam lost track of time. He didn't know how much longer he could keep going. His hands were numb, his forearms were beginning to cramp up. Still no sign of Pipaluk. The enemy was not the sea or the wind. The enemy was fear, cold, fatigue and loneliness.

A pointed bow edged into view on his left.

'Pipaluk! Are you all right?' he bawled above the din of wind and wave.

She grinned. 'How are you?'

'Glad to see you!'

His heart lifted. He had new energy. He knew he was going to make it to the other side.

They slept for a long time. When Adam woke he looked out to sea and was thankful to be safe on land. The gale was still blowing. He became aware of Pipaluk's thigh pressing against him. He gazed into her sleeping face. Through shared adventures and danger they had learned to trust their lives to each other. Loving her was no longer something to run from. It was what he wanted more than anything else. He wanted to make love to her, but he wanted to be sure it was for the right reason – not so that he could boast to Skug about it if he ever saw him again, or because he was greedy for some new sensation. He remembered the note of scorn in Qortoq's voice when he'd said that many whalers who took Inuit women never came back to them. He did not want to be like that. It was not what his father had done. If he found his father... When he found him, they'd probably return to England as soon as possible. Adam imagined the two of them walking side by side in a London park, or visiting Aunt Emily's grave together. But how could he leave Pipaluk? How could he wrench himself away from this beautiful land? Adam rolled away from the warm, desirable body next to him and pulled on his boots. They were out of food. He'd go hunting, that's what he'd do. Fishing was their usual standby, towing a line with hook and bait for Arctic cod, char and pollock. There was no chance of that today. He picked up the bow and left the shelter.

Several hours later, he returned empty-handed. He'd fired an arrow at a ptarmigan on the ground and missed it. Then he'd seen a hare and missed that too. 'Even famous hunters miss sometimes,' Pipaluk assured him.

Adam noticed that her eyes were red.

'Did you wear your goggles yesterday? Your eyes look...'

'Oh... I... I'm not sure. Maybe not.'

Pipaluk set rabbit snares. The next day and the next the wind was as strong as ever. The snares yielded nothing and again Adam was unsuccessful with the bow.

'When I should have been learning about the ways of rabbits, I was in England learning the ways of the qallunaat,' Pipaluk said. 'Not that there's much difference!' she added, trying to force a grin.

Adam could see the hunger in her eyes. His own stomach was clenching in protest at its emptiness.

Weak with hunger, Adam set out yet again with the bow to hunt by the midnight sun. Barren scree slopes led to a plateau which was a mixture of bare rock, patches of snow and stretches of low, scrubby dwarf willow and birch. Everywhere there were little lakes and pools of water, brimming with cloud and sky. In sheltered spots were tiny meadows, bright with Arctic flowers. Adam didn't know what any of them were, except one was some kind of poppy and another was what he imagined cotton should look like. He walked with his body bowed to the wind, but eyes alert for anything that moved. He walked for several miles, seeing nothing, shivering because there was no food inside him. He felt dizzy. Sometimes colours faded and everything was just black and white dots. He stopped to rest. Carried on the wind was a clicking sound, like a thousand Aunt Emilys knitting.

Cautiously he topped the rise and saw a forest of antlers, a herd of several hundred caribou. He was above and downwind of them. The clicking came from their ankle-bones, which they used to communicate with each other. Adam began to crawl forward. Slowly, very slowly, he inched down the slope. Another ten yards and he would be within range of the nearest caribou. It looked up from its grazing. He lay still, head down. It resumed feeding. Another yard forward . . . his knee caught a finely balanced boulder, sending it rumbling down the slope. The herd took flight. In less than a minute they were far up a different slope, alert and wary. Adam nearly wept with frustration. A hare, disturbed by the fleeing herd, was loping straight towards him. It stopped only a few yards from him. Very slowly he raised his bow and released the arrow. The hare bounded in the air and darted off. Thirty yards on, it fell dead.

Adam was so overcome with excitement that, when he reached the hare, he had to sit down. There was enough meat on it to make a good meal for two. Adam thought, If I cut it open and take the guts out it will be much lighter. . . . which would, of course, leave the liver and heart lying loose . . . and best eaten raw on the spot . . . without sharing them with Pipaluk. Ashamed, he jumped up and began the weary trudge back to their shelter. It was Inuit custom, wasn't it, for the hunter to take the best bits? He could eat it all, in fact, and never tell her. He broke into a stumbling run, singing, shouting . . . anything to drown out the voice of temptation. He stopped for another rest. Suppose he just tore off a leg and gnawed on that? He plunged down the scree slope, the shelter in sight. Pipaluk was waving and then shouting congratulations as she saw the hare.

Pipaluk lit a fire by sparking flints over dry moss and then feeding it the woody cassiope plant which carpeted the valley. She stirred the stew in the pot and sang:

The Great Sun has set me in motion,
Set me adrift
And I move as a weed in the river.
The arch of sky
And mightiness of storms
Encompasses me
And I am left
Trembling with joy.

Adam sat with his mouth watering, while the stew bubbled, feeling triumphant and guilty by turns. He told Pipaluk how he had nearly given in to temptation and eaten the hare all by himself.

'Can you forgive me?'

'There is nothing to forgive, Adam.' She stroked his face. 'Thank you for telling me. And thank you for bringing meat to the pot.'

They kissed and clung to each other.

'I think the stew is ready,' Adam said, breaking away.

After the most wonderful meal he could ever remember, they slept.

Pipaluk was out tending her traps when Adam woke. He crawled out of the shelter. The wind had dropped to a mere breeze. A man was striding along the ridge above. A kayak was slung by the cockpit over his shoulder. Most likely, thought Adam, he was portaging his light craft from one side of the peninsula to the other, rather than paddle the twenty miles or so round the headland. There was something different about the man. Adam studied the retreating figure. Now he saw what it was – the man was much taller than most Inuit! The man stopped, put down his kayak and half turned. His hood was down and Adam could see he had a mop of white curly hair and a white beard.

'Father!' Adam shouted. 'Father! Nathaniel! Terrianiaq! It's me, Adam!'

The man didn't hear him, nor was he looking in the right direction. Adam shouted and waved until the man disappeared down the other side of the ridge.

His lungs bursting, Adam scrambled towards the ridge. He arrived at the top in time to see the man . . . his father launching the kayak from the shore below. Adam shouted till he was hoarse, but his father's back was turned and the waves breaking on the beach were loud in his ears. Adam turned. He must follow his father. He needed to get back to the shelter and the kayaks. He almost hurled himself down the slope, running, slithering, jumping. His mind raced. Every minute counted. All the time his father was getting further and further away. If he set off in his kayak on his own, it would mean leaving Pipaluk behind and she wouldn't know where he had gone. What if something happened to her? They had only survived in this wild and dangerous country by protecting and caring for each other. Whom did he want most – his father or Pipaluk? He groaned aloud.

'I don't know!' he screamed into the air. 'How can I choose? How can I possibly choose?'

Chapter Twenty-Seven

'I have seen the dog with two heads!' Pipaluk shouted as Adam ran up to the shelter. 'Remember what my uncle said? A two-headed dog guards the entrance to the sea caves. I have seen a big rock just like that!'

Adam collapsed on the ground, panting hard.

'What's the matter, Adam?'

Adam pointed towards the ridge he had just descended. 'I... think I saw... my father. No, it was definitely him.'

Suddenly Adam knew the answer to his terrible dilemma. Qortoq had said the caves went right through to the other side. If they could find the way through, it would be much quicker than either carrying a kayak over the ridge or paddling round the headland.

'Quick, get ready to go. We haven't a moment to lose!'

While they bundled things up and shoved them into the kayaks, Adam told Pipaluk what had happened. She, in turn, related how she had been inspecting one of her snares further round the bay when she had noticed the rock at the base of some sea cliffs.

'Look, you can see it from here. From this angle you don't see the two heads. But from further round they snarl at you.'

'I was so close to being with him again! So close!' Adam groaned as they carried the kayaks to the water's edge.

'If only he had looked in my direction!'

'But, Adam, you've actually seen him! Now you know he's alive and that he's here.'

'You're right. I should be happy. It's just that . . . well, it's so frustrating. If only—'

'And another thing, Adam. If he was carrying his kayak, it couldn't have been heavily loaded, which means he can't be far from home.'

They paddled towards the tall guardian rock.

Adam said, 'You'd never guess there was anything behind it. Are you sure?'

'No, but I'm sure about the two heads. Look, there's one of them . . . the eyes, and the jaws.'

'Yes, I see them. Let's hope your uncle's right about the rest of it.'

They heard the cave before they saw it – a hollow panting as if there was a wounded Minotaur crouching somewhere in its depths. The swell piled up against the dog rock before funnelling into the cave with a roar, only to swash out again minutes later. Adam and Pipaluk hovered close to the narrow passage between the rock and the cave mouth, back-paddling so as not to be swept in out of control. They manoeuvred their kayaks, waiting for the right moment.

'I'll go first,' Adam called out.

Between the churning chaos of the outgoing water and the roaring surge of the next incoming swell was a moment of calm.

'Now!' Pipaluk shouted.

As Adam entered the cave there was a flurry of wings overhead. Half a dozen alarmed puffins zoomed out. Every drip from the vaulted ceiling, every sucking and gurgling sound was magnified into booming echoes. The next swell swept in, blotting out the light from the entrance. Higher and higher rose Adam's kayak as the wave filled the cave. Adam could feel the pressure in his ears as the air compressed. Then he was battling to prevent himself being washed out again as water cascaded from ledges and the cave half emptied. Pipaluk joined him, exclaiming in amazement, her words reverberating around the high chamber. They moved forward in the dim light, making use of the calm intervals and trying to hold their own during the bits when it seemed all Hell had broken loose. At the far end of the outer chamber the cave roof was much lower. Up they rose again as another swell flooded in. Adam was sure his head was going to bang against the rocky roof. He flattened himself along the deck. He felt his back press against the rock. Only about a foot of airspace was left. Then the wave fell away, sloshing and swirling out of the cave. They bumped and scraped round a corner into complete darkness. Adam had never met total and absolute darkness before. He could not see his own hand in front of his face.

'Pipaluk, are you there?'

'Yes.'

He guessed from the echoes that this was a smaller, narrower chamber. Being cut off from the force of the swell, it was calmer. Afraid of bumping his head, Adam inched cautiously into the blackness. He kept one wall within touching distance of his paddle. Their hissing breath, the loud dripping, the water sobbing in cracks and fissures filled the darkness with eerie noises. Adam felt the reassuring bump of Pipaluk's bows against his stern.

'I'm glad you're with me, Pipaluk.'

'Same here.'

'He could be miles away by now.'

'On the other hand, he might have hauled up for a rest, or stopped because he's harpooned a seal or something. You never know.'

The cave walls were closing in. Adam's paddle was clashing against them on both sides now. Then there wasn't enough room to paddle and he was pushing his kayak along with his hands against the cold, wet walls. The cave broadened out again into a third chamber. Something luminous glowed above their heads.

Behind him Pipaluk said, 'Am I imagining it, or is it getting lighter?'

'You mean these glowing things?'

'No. I mean . . . In front of my eyes it's not like the raven, it's more like a wolf in its summer coat.'

They felt their way, with slithering hands, round another corner. Somewhere in the distance was a faint slit of light. As they paddled towards it, it grew wider and taller. Beyond it the open sea was rising and falling.

'We did it!' Adam whooped, as they emerged on the other side of the peninsula. His eyes searched the sea for another kayak bobbing up and down.

'Can you see anything, Pipaluk?'

'No, sorry... Wait! I thought I saw... No, it's gone... Yes, there it is!'

Every now and then a black speck would appear. They watched for the tell-tale flash of a paddle blade.

'I see it!' Pipaluk cried. 'A kayak. No doubt about it!'

'It's him! It's my father! It's got to be!'

Adam and Pipaluk paddled with all their strength in an attempt to close the gap between themselves and the distant kayaker. But the paddler, whoever he was, disappeared into a channel between the mainland and a large island.

When they reached the mouth of the channel, the flood tide was rushing through the narrow passage like a river in full torrent. Adam's father had gone through it close to slack water. Adam and Pipaluk, however, had arrived at the same spot over half an hour later – time enough for the current to pick up speed. They both knew that the sensible thing would be to wait the six hours till the next slack water. And they both knew they were not going to wait.

'Let's go!' Pipaluk yelled, sending her kayak surging forward into the current.

Eddies caught at them, whirling them round. Blisters of water welled up, as impenetrable as a wall. The shores on either side flashed by at an unbelievable speed. In front of Adam a whirlpool was growing bigger and bigger, its dark, spiralling vortex gurgling horribly. Adam paddled frantically out of its way. Minutes later, they were squirted out at the other end to drift in quieter water, panting and elated. Adam looked into Pipaluk's shining eyes, sharing the moment with her.

Immediately ahead of them was a whole cluster of islands and a maze of different channels winding between them.

'Your father could have taken any one of them,' Pipaluk said dejectedly.

They tried to pick out what looked like the main channel through the middle of the cluster and follow that.

Adam fought the lump in his throat. 'We can't have lost him! Not now!'

Pipaluk drew level with him and clutched his arm. She was pointing. On the biggest island in the archipelago, beside a stream, was a caribou tent.

They landed on the nearest beach. The wind had died down. The mosquitoes and blackfly were out in force. With their kayaking skins still on, sealed against the voracious horde, and fanning their faces with squares of sealskin, Adam and Pipaluk ventured into the blackly shimmering air. So dense were the mosquitoes that it was like twilight. With so much meltwater turning the stream into a torrent, it was difficult to find a place to cross. Finally, they approached the tent. Cuts of meat dangled from a pole, and caribou hides were slung over a line, drying in the sun. Four tethered dogs loudly announced their arrival.

A whole family tumbled out of the tent. None of them was Nathaniel Jones. Kutlok, his wife, his brother and two children greeted them warmly and immediately started preparing food. Adam allowed himself to be led into the tent, accepting that, for the moment, the trail had gone cold. It might be better to learn what the family knew rather than continue searching blindly.

Adam was thankful for the smoky interior of the tent which kept the mosquitoes at bay. This was their summer camp, they said, where they came to hunt caribou and ptarmigan. There followed the usual long exchange of names of each other's ancestors. It was the first time Adam had ever told anyone that his mother was Salamina from Nuusuaq. Who her parents and grandparents were, he had no idea. He wished he knew.

To Adam's surprise, the first dish served up consisted of vegetables. Not that the fermented contents of a caribou's stomach were the sort of vegetables he'd ever had before. But mixed with digested willow buds from a ptarmigan's gizzard, they tasted good. Kutlok went out and dug from the snow handfuls of frozen eider duck eggs which he'd cached. They were eaten crisp and hard, like apples. Next came roasted caribou haunch. It was a kind of venison, Adam supposed. It tasted like a cross between turkey and beef, but less fatty.

While they ate, Adam and Pipaluk talked about their search for Nathaniel.

'Have you ever seen the quallunaat they call Terrianiaq?' Adam asked Kutlok.

He shook his head. 'We are only here for the short summer.'

Later, when they could cram in no more food, Kutlok said to Adam, 'There is something I want to show you and your wife.'

Adam and Pipaluk exchanged shy glances, thrilled and happy.

'It's some kind of qallunaat magic spell,' Kutlok was saying. 'Perhaps you can explain it to me.'

From the back of the tent he produced a leather-bound book. On it, in gold lettering, were the words 'Logbook of the Whaling Ship, *Triton*'.

Kutlok spoke about how he had exchanged it for a bearskin with a man who had exchanged it for two narwhal horns with a man who had found it in a small, battered wooden boat, along with three dead qallunaat.

Adam, his heart leaping about inside his chest, was hardly able to keep himself from snatching the book from Kutlok's hands. He explained in a trembling voice that the little black marks all over the page were like the spoor of an animal. They told a story if you knew how to look at them properly.

'Tell us the story!' they chorused.

Adam told them about the wreck of the *Triton*. They were keenly interested. They wanted every detail. They wanted to go over it again and again, speculating, discussing. What Adam wanted was to seize the book and run to some quiet spot where he could read it in privacy. He offered his shotgun in exchange for the book. The two brothers conferred. They agreed to come with him to where the kayaks were beached and inspect the gun.

They had heard about guns, but never seen one. Adam told them it wouldn't work without cartridges. They shrugged as if this was of little importance.

At last, Adam sat beneath the kayaks in the little shelter he and Pipaluk had made. The *Triton*'s logbook was propped on his knees. He skipped through the pages until he saw the name of Nathaniel Jones and began reading.

Chapter Twenty-Eight

Two days after leaving Kutlok and his family, Adam and Pipaluk were still searching for Nathaniel, paddling on a rolling sea amongst shining, dancing chunks of ice. The coastline was indented and complex. They had barely gone a mile directly northwards in two days. It had taken them all this time to look into all the fjords and their offshoots.

'The big fjords have little fjords off them,' Adam complained. 'And even they have side bits!'

It was a beautiful day, with white clouds chasing across the sky. If Adam hadn't been so concerned about finding his father, he would have been enjoying himself. A rolling wave picked up his kayak and carried it forward. He balanced on the crest before surfing down the front of the wave like an arrow released from a bow. If you could avoid hitting a piece of ice, there could be no better way to travel, he thought.

'Except by sledge, on smooth ice, under a full moon,' Pipaluk said in one of the times they shared the same wave.

'He must be somewhere here,' Adam said. 'Do you suppose we've been past the place and missed it?'

'I don't think so. You couldn't help seeing great big red cliffs, could you?'

'I'm not sure. Perhaps you could.'

Despite his concern, Adam also felt an enormous sense of relief. For months and months the question had nagged at the back of his mind – when his father survived the ordeal on the ice floe, why hadn't he returned to England? Didn't his father love him enough to want to be with him as soon as possible? The *Triton*'s logbook had made a number of references to the harpooner, the spectioneer Nathaniel Jones, and how his heavy drinking was becoming an increasing problem. On several occasions he had been too drunk to do his job properly. According to the logbook, he had purloined ten bottles of rum from the stores and was in possession of them when he had drifted away on the ice. Qortoq had said that Terrianiaq was a man wrestling with demons. That was the answer. His father had been ashamed to return to him until he had overcome the demon alcohol. He had gone north, away from the whaling ships and trading posts where he could indulge his fondness for drink. He had done it because he cared what his son thought of him and wanted to return to him a sober man.

Adam and Pipaluk drew their kayaks alongside each other and formed a raft while they drank from the waterskin which had been keeping warm beneath Pipaluk's anorak and ate the slices of ptarmigan Kutlok had given them.

Adam said, 'Do you remember those cans of grouse, reserved for officers only?... Well, ptarmigan is a kind of grouse.'

'And ours isn't out of a can.'

'I hope they're rescued... When we... Horse and Skug and me... when we came hunting with you and

Qortoq . . . Do you think your uncle ever meant to return? Was it all a plan to get us away from what he thought was a death march?'

'Not at first, Adam. If there had been seals to catch, food to bring back to the others, he would have done so. He thought up the plan after we had set out.'

'You knew about it, then?'

'Yes.'

'You didn't tell me.'

'Would you have agreed if you had known?'

'I don't know.'

Adam looked behind him. An iceberg, catching more wind than they were, was overtaking them. They watched it, till they were sure it wouldn't pass too close. Adam felt certain that, as long as he lived, he would never cease to thrill at the sight of these magical creations. On his other side were spectacular cliffs and peaks with the top of the icecap just visible beyond, its glimmer reflected on the underside of the clouds. He felt alive here in a way he had never done in England. He had learned from the Inuit how to live at the heart of the moment.

'Greenland feels like a song inside me,' he told her.

She smiled at him. 'There's an old Inuit saying that all songs are born in man out in the great wilderness.'

'This song was born in me when I met you, Pipaluk.'

To have experienced so much, to have seen such wonders of nature, to have met Pipaluk . . . what more could he ask for? To find his father – that was what was missing.

Adam laid a hand on Pipaluk's arm. 'Kutlok said he'd been coming to this area, every summer, for years. Yet he has never seen my father.'

'Have you seen a fox or a wolf or a musk ox since you have been in this land?'

'No.'

'But they are here, all the same.'

Soon after they had started paddling again, the triangular fins of half a dozen or more orcas, or killer whales, sliced through the water, parallel to them and keeping pace with them. Seen from under the surface, a kayak might be mistaken for a seal or a narwhal which the ferocious orcas hunted. A long, dark shape flitted beneath Adam's hull. Pipaluk quickly sized up the situation. Capsizing her kayak, she cupped her hands and imitated the roar of a bull walrus. The fins veered sharply away and sped off in another direction.

'Well done!' Adam called to Pipaluk as she rolled upright.

'Watch out!' she shouted.

Two orcas were bearing down on Adam, obviously with the intention of squashing him between them, the way they did with seals. Again Pipaluk capsized and gave her walrus roar. The orcas changed course, but did not flee as before. About two hundred yards away was a fjord with a shallow entrance. It was one they had searched two days ago. If they could cross the shallows, the orcas would not be able to follow.

The two kayakers sprinted for safety. The orcas turned and tore through the waves towards them. Adam felt his paddle touch shingle. The orcas swerved and headed out to deep water again.

'Too close for comfort!' Adam panted. 'We could have been some orca's lunchtime sandwich!'

'I bet I would have tasted better than you!'

They landed on the other side of the shallows.

Adam gave a cry of astonishment. 'Red cliffs! I... I don't understand!'

Pipaluk stared at them in disbelief. 'They weren't there two days ago.'

'We couldn't possibly have missed them.'

'And it's definitely the same fjord, Adam. How could this happen?'

Adam scratched his head. 'I remember all that bit as being a steep snow slope.'

They stood, unable to take their eyes off this inexplicable sight. Smoke drifted into view.

They continued to stare until, finally, Pipaluk let out a shriek. 'Smoke!'

'What?'

'Smoke, Adam! Smoke! An igloo, cooking, people!'

They ran towards the source of the smoke. Topping a small rise, they looked down into a sheltered hollow. In it was what was obviously a deserted village... except for the one igloo from which smoke was rising from a hole in the roof. A man was sitting outside it.

'Uunarpoq,' said the man, commenting politely on the weather, as was the custom.

He was looking at Adam with an uncertain, hesitant

expression in his eyes. He pulled back his hood. He had curly white hair and a white beard.

'Father! Father, it's me, Adam!'

'Dear God, I wasn't sure. Here, in the Arctic!'

Their arms were around each other. Adam's face was buried in his chest. Tears of relief and happiness welled up.

In Nathaniel Jones's igloo, they feasted and talked and talked and feasted and talked some more. Adam told the whole story from the time of Aunt Emily's death onwards. Nathaniel shed a tear at his sister's death, growled angrily at the meanness of his brother, Jeremiah, and exclaimed several times what a good friend Elisha was. Pipaluk nudged Adam and pointed to the large whaling harpoon in the corner, the same one as in his photograph, the same one which had killed the bear on the ice floe. While Nathaniel roared with laughter at the idea of being the subject of a string figure, a legendary person, Adam's eyes darted into every corner of the igloo, looking for evidence of rum, whisky or whalers' moonshine, and saw none.

When Adam had finished his tale, Nathaniel said, 'I'm proud of you, Adam. Very proud. And you, young lady – I can see he would never have managed without you.'

His father had changed, Adam thought, and yet he was still the same.

Nathaniel said, 'It is true what you read about me in the *Triton*'s logbook. I haven't touched a drop of drink since the day I killed the bear on the ice floe. Somehow it brought me face to face with myself. It was like I had been given another life, another chance, as if I had been born again.'

Nathaniel served up seal meat cooked with herbs and wildflowers, then resumed his tale.

'I still had six bottles of rum with me. I poured the lot into the sea. That wasn't the end of it by a long chalk. Once I got to land there was no lack of opportunity for backsliding. It was hard, Adam, harder than surviving on an ice floe, much harder... But I beat it. I did it for myself, but most of all, I did it for you.'

Before he and Adam found each other, Nathaniel said, he had already decided the time had come for him to return to England and to his son.

'For more than two years I thought you were dead!' Adam cried in anguish and there was accusation in his voice, too.

Nathaniel drew his son close. 'I know and I'm sorry. Believe me, you would have wished me dead if you'd seen how low I'd sunk. I would have been no father to you.'

Adam rested his head on his father's chest. England, his father had said. But what about Pipaluk? She had only just returned to her own people. She had been miserable in England. He couldn't ask her to come with him. He didn't want to go without her. As a matter of fact, he didn't want to go at all. He wanted to stay in this new, exciting land. But if his father wanted to go back... Adam felt as if he was being torn in two. Was he, after all, going to have to decide between them?

Next morning Nathaniel took Adam to see his mother's grave. There was a simple wooden board, which looked as though it had once been part of a boat. On it was carved, 'Salamina, beloved wife of Nathaniel and loving mother of Adam.'

'No dates,' Nathaniel said. 'This land is timeless. Nothing decays, including memories.'

Adam collected Arctic flowers and placed them on the grave.

Nathaniel put a hand on his son's shoulder. 'I can see Pipaluk means as much to you as Salamina . . . as your mother . . . meant to me.'

Adam bit his lip and remained silent.

Nathaniel continued, 'Taking her as my wife was one of the best things I ever did. I just wish I had spent more time with her. Instead of going off whaling I should have—'

'I don't want to leave Pipaluk!' Adam burst out. 'But, if you want to return to England . . .'

'Want to? I don't. I'm only going so that I can be with you.'

'But I don't want to go either! I want to stay here.'

Nathaniel laughed – a big, hearty laugh, the way Adam remembered him laughing. 'Well, I'm glad we got that straight! You'd better tell Pipaluk and put her out of her misery.'

'Oh, Adam!' Pipaluk cried, flushing all over and throwing herself into his arms.

They hugged and kissed and danced around the outside of the igloo, beaming at each other.

'I am so happy, Adam!'

'Me too.'

That afternoon they set out in their kayaks, heading south.

'Tell us about the red cliffs, Nathaniel,' Pipaluk said. She explained their utter mystification.

Nathaniel laughed. 'It happens sometimes at this time of year. It's some kind of wind-borne plant or lichen. It settles on the snow and thrives on the reflected light, turning the snow red. Quite rare, I believe, but this is one of those places.'

The return journey to Narlok had its share of adventure, hardship and danger, but somehow, Adam thought, it seemed easier with three of them, particularly when he was in love with one of them and the other was his father. As they paddled they talked about their hopes for the future. Nathaniel said he did not want to return to the whaling life. Part of the reason he had started drinking heavily was because he had become disillusioned with whaling. It was no longer a fair contest between man and whale.

'The more I learnt about whales, Adam, the less I wanted to kill them . . . not in that way . . . not with the new explosive harpoons. I want nothing to do with them.'

'My uncle, Qortoq, would agree with you,' Pipaluk said.

Nathaniel nodded. 'Eating away at me all the time was the thought that, in a hundred different ways, I was helping to destroy the way of life that had been Salamina's.'

In a break for a rest and a snack, they sat overlooking a deep green sea in which icebergs pirouetted in the current.

Nathaniel said, 'During this last year, I changed my mind about something. Experiencing the Arctic from the deck of a whaler is not the same as being really close to it. Instead of seeing it as a conflict between man and the Arctic, or Nathaniel Jones against the whales, I began to understand what the Inuit have always known, what I am sure you, Adam, have discovered, that we are a part of these things.'

Adam nodded his head thoughtfully. 'I don't think I could have put it into words, but everything Qortoq and Pipaluk have taught me has been saying that in one way or another.'

He and Salamina, Nathaniel said, had talked about living together in Greenland. They had dreamed about building a little house which would be both Inuit and qallunaat, and about finding a way of life that combined good things from both worlds.

'That's what we've been thinking, isn't it, Pipaluk?' Adam cried.

Adam told his father about Qortoq's harpoon which had an iron point made in Birmingham and a shaft made of narwhal horn.

'Qortoq said that Inuit and qallunaat together was best.'

'Best for harpoons and best for sons,' Nathaniel said, ruffling Adam's hair.

'The crevasse,' Pipaluk said. 'Tell your father about

bridging the gap between the two sides. Tell him how what made the bridge was Inuit and qallunaat things both together.'

'That's right,' Adam said. 'It was . . . it was like you and me joined together, Pipaluk.'

Pipaluk took a breath as if about to say something, then fidgeted with her boot.

Adam looked at her. 'What is it, my love?'

'I think I should tell you about two of Qortoq's visions.'

When Qortoq paddled twenty-three days to intercept the *Prince Consort*, it was not to meet Pipaluk, although this was a secondary reason. It was to meet Adam. In a trance he had seen a qallunaat ship carrying a boy, a young man, who was both qallunaat and Inuit. Adam had turned into a rainbow, arching across the sky, bridging the gap between the lands of the Inuit and the qallunaat. The vision had told the angakok of Narlok that this special person was in great danger and might be lost to them unless he went to him and protected him.

'Then my uncle had a second vision – you know, Adam – on the *Prince Consort*, when he was flogged.'

In this vision, Pipaluk said, Qortoq had been shown terrible things. He had seen animals killed in their thousands by guns, slaughtered without respect. He had seen his people attacked by the same demon that Terrianiaq fought. The ice had begun to melt so that Nanok, the bear, went away, never to be seen again. And poisonous winds from the land of the qallunaat had brought death to his beautiful country. When he saw these things, Qortoq knew that if the Inuit were to heed the warning and prevent them from happening, they needed Adam and people like him to act as a bridge between the two worlds.

'Just before we left to look for you, Nathaniel, my uncle told me something else.'

'What was that?' father and son asked in unison.

'He told me that the first vision he ever had, the one he had in the dark cave, was this same vision.'

By the time they rounded the final headland and Narlok came into sight, Nathaniel, Adam and Pipaluk were agreed that they could not stop change happening. The moment white men had arrived off the coast of Greenland, change had been inevitable. What might make that change beneficial and not harmful was the advice and guidance of people who understood the ways of both qallunaat and Inuit, who spoke the languages of both and who acted, not from greed and desire for profit, but from love of the people and of the land.

'Do you see what I see?' Pipaluk said.

Pulled up on the beach below Narlok was a forty-foot naval cutter. On the cliff above was a group of figures waving. Among them were two who were dressed like qallunaat.

Horse and Skug were standing on the beach waiting for them. Adam leapt out of his kayak and ran towards them. They shook hands, then shook hands again and thumped each other on the back. Adam introduced his father. They walked up the path to the village, talking nonstop. Adam didn't need to be told that the cutter was part of a rescue mission.

'Have the others been found?' was his first question.

'Yes. Only twelve survived, I'm afraid.'

'Ferret? Captain McLellan?'

'Both alive, Adam. The ship's surgeon had to amputate Elisha's leg, though. Ferret, like the others, is weak and badly frostbitten, but he'll recover.'

Quisby was also one of the survivors, but not Bumble Burden. He had left a note saying he was on a heroic trek to the North Pole and that he would be back for afternoon tea and to be sure to tell Nanny to make potted meat sandwiches. He was never seen again.

The cutter's crew of ten seamen had set up tents beside the village. Many of the families of Narlok had gone to summer camps, but Qortoq was there and old Arnajark.

Horse said, 'When Qortoq told me where you had gone and that you would be coming back, I decided to wait for you here.'

Adam nodded his agreement. 'Too big a chance that, amongst all the islands and inlets, we'd pass each other without knowing it.'

Pipaluk told Qortoq that Adam and Nathaniel would not be returning to England. Qortoq's wrinkled face radiated delight.

'Now the red fox can stop running,' he said. 'Now an old angakok can rest and be happy.'

In Qortoq's igloo, over bowls of tea and pickled walrus liver, the recently promoted First Lieutenant George Grenier, otherwise known as Horse, unfolded his story.

He and Skug had travelled to the south of Greenland, which was ice-free, and had managed to get a Danish ship back to Copenhagen and then another ship to London. As soon as possible, the Admiralty had mounted a rescue mission for the crew of the *Prince Consort*.

'We was the first to volunteer,' Skug said.

Skug was now an assistant in the engine room, with every prospect of making it to Petty Officer one day. In the months travelling together, Horse had taught him a great deal. He was able to read and write to a good standard and his knowledge of mathematics, navigation and engineering would stand him in good stead.

Skug grinned. 'No call for an engineer to be climbing the rigging, see.'

On the way through Davis Strait they had met an American whaler which had reported a strange sight. Through their telescopes they had seen a party of British naval officers, in full regalia, sitting down to dinner on an ice floe in the middle of nowhere and not another ship in sight. Horse paused in his narrative to produce a bottle of rum from his pocket and pass it round. Adam was pleased at the ease with which his father refused it. Qortoq also brought out a bottle. He had saved it for a special occasion, he said. He took a long swig before offering round an ornate bottle containing a bright blue substance – Horse's eau de Cologne.

Pipaluk slipped out of the igloo to fetch more food from the cache, her hand caressing Adam's neck as she went by, a quiet smile passing between them.

Horse said they had found the survivors sailing two of the boats down the coast of Baffin Island. Before the ice broke up, while they were still hauling the boats, they had come across a savssat – an open lead into which whales and narwhals swim and then get trapped when the lead closes again. Over forty narwhals had been packed into an ever-decreasing area of open water, fighting for space and air, their bodies vertical, horns pointing to the sky. The crew had killed all the animals they wanted. By then, though, thirty men were already dead. Another two died from eating too much too quickly and seven more died later, either from gangrene or simply worn down by the ordeal. They had remained beside the site of the savssat with the carcasses of the animals they had slain until the ice broke up and they were afloat.

After the rescue of the survivors, Horse had been put in charge of the ship's cutter with orders to sail up the coast of Greenland, looking for Adam.

'So, Adam, all I have to do now is take you back with me... and your father, of course.'

'We're not coming,' Adam said. 'We have decided to stay here.'

'Are you sure?'

'I have never been more sure about anything in my life.'

Nathaniel said, 'Please tell Elisha that Adam and I are very grateful to him . . . and . . . and we were sorry to hear about his leg.'

'I will.'

Adam added, 'And tell Ferret his lucky amulet worked. It saved me from being eaten by a bear.'

Skug said, 'I was looking forward to you and me together, Adam . . . you know . . . on the way back. Could of had a right laugh.' He grinned. 'Was a time I'd never have believed I'd hear myself say that! You was the best back-end of a cow I never saw!'

'Thanks, Skug. And you sang better than any cow I ever did hear.'

'Good luck to you, Adam.'

'And to you, Skug. Who knows, we may meet again.'

'Yeah, I might be back this way, you never know.'

'Or we might come to England one spring . . . to see the trees in leaf and smell the new-mown hay.'

Outside the igloo, Pipaluk was singing softly to herself.

Glorious is life
Now I am filled with joy
For every time a dawn
Makes white the sky of night
For every time the sun goes up
Over the heavens.